JENNY KISSED ME!

by

Thomas Allen

Copyright © 2014 by Thomas Allen
All rights reserved.

Available from Amazon.com and other retail markets.

No part of this publication may be reproduced, distributed or transmitted in any form, or by any means including photocopying, recording or other electronic or mechanical methods, without prior written permission of the publisher, except in the case of brief quotations embodied in critical reviews and certain other noncommercial uses permitted by copyright law.

This is a work of fiction. Though some events are based on real happenings, and some names of characters are drawn from the author's past acquaintances, there is no intended association between an actual happening and the name of the person connected with it. Characters have been fictionalized as a product of the author's imagination. Locales are sometimes used for atmospheric purposes.

Cover design © 2014 E. Franklin Miller

Library of Congress Control Number:2014910596
CreateSpace Independent Publishing Platform, North Charleston, SC

ISBN: 13:978-1497450356
ISBN: 10:1497450357

THE FOUR LOVES by C.S. Lewis copyright © C.S. Lewis Pte. Ltd. 1960. Extract reprinted by permission.

Excerpts from **THE FOUR LOVES** by C. S. Lewis. Copyright© C. S. Lewis, 1960, renewed 1988 by Arthur Owen Barfield. Reprinted by permission of Houghton Mifflin Harcourt Publishing Company. All rights reserved.

I Said My Pajamas (And Put On My Pray'rs)

Words and Music by Eddie Pola and George Wyle
Copyright©1949,1950 UNIVERSAL MUSIC CORP
Copyright Renewed
All Rights Reserved Used by Permission
Reprinted by Permission of Hal Leonard Corporation

"All I Have To Do Is Dream" written by Boudleaux ©1958 by House of Bryant Publications (renewed) All Rights Reserved Used by Permission

"Summertime Love" written by Head, Gibson, Bolton, Frazier, Buie, Pennington, Majority Interest in composition and recording copyright© held by D&R Sales and Service, LLC All Rights Reserved Used by Permission

Scripture quotations marked (CEV) are from the Contemporary English Version Copyright © 1991,1992,1995 by American Bible Society, Used by Permission.

Other scripture from The King James Version of the Bible.

To Elaine,

my wife and inspiration

This book could not have been

written without you.

...The passion of love bursting into flame is more powerful than death, stronger than the grave. Love cannot be drowned by oceans or floods; it cannot be bought, no matter what is offered.

Song of Songs (CEV)

JENNY KISSED ME!

ONE

The Shoebox

Anticipation heightened as Jenny's flight began circling the celebrated Manhattan skyline. It was her first ever glimpse of the Big Apple. *Imagine…I'm seeing the most famous city in the United States…probably the whole world.*

The lyrics of a song popped into her mind. That frequently happened, given her affinity for Easy Listening music. She heard it clearly—Frank Sinatra's signature hit, "New York, New York." The line about making a brand new start lingered. *That is exactly what I'm doing. I'll tell Sandra all about it.* The song stopped playing in her mind when she heard the pilot's voice. "We will have a slight delay, landing at Newark in twenty minutes."

It was six days before the Millennium. Jenny was on her way to Rome. From the moment she boarded the plane at DFW Airport three and a half hours earlier, she was filled with anticipation. She would get to see her best friend for the first time in two decades. The thought of being together again came with a slight apprehension. *What if, after all these years, I don't even recognize her at the airport?*

Sandra lived in the northeast since the late 1960s and missed their thirty-year class reunion, nine years earlier. Newark, New Jersey was a long way from San Marcos, Texas where the two of them grew up. As Jenny thought about the last class reunion, she giggled about the nametags. They were invaluable. In her late forties at that time, she wore glasses for reading purposes only. At the reunion, she left them in her purse, hoping she could recognize her old classmates. Most of the time it did not work. In fact, it rarely did. After a couple of failed attempts, she decided to hold her glasses in her hand, having them available once the initial glance proved fruitless. It turned out to be fun. She would approach someone, quickly put on her glasses and then read the nametag, exclaiming, "Oh Paige, it's you." They would both laugh.

It amazed her how everyone had changed. *Surely, I haven't...not that much...well, except for my short blonde hair.*

However, Jenny's *life* had changed since her happy school days. In the last few years, she found herself frequently wanting to revisit those times. She had been doing just that most of the plane ride. Her early years, in contrast with her life since, were the best. Reflections on those days had a way of erasing some of the pain, if only for a short time.

JENNY KISSED ME!

The happiest remembrance took her to a boy, a time, and a happening. His name was Jonathan, she was fourteen, and the occasion was in English class. He was a new student and even though she had a class with him, she didn't know he existed until about a month into the school year. When she did become aware of him, it became the most memorable moment of those wonderful school years. Jonathan stood by the teacher's desk and recited a romantic poem while he looked right at her. After he finished, from that moment on whenever she saw him she recalled the day, the poem, and the feeling, though she never told him about it. In time, high school ended. She went away to college and the memory of him waned.

Years passed and Jenny married. More years passed and she married again. She thought of Jonathan occasionally, but only in fleeting moments.

Five months ago, as she prepared to move into a new home, the memories returned—in torrents. Jenny was in her bedroom closet sorting through boxes and books retrieved four years earlier from her mother's home after her death. Determined to reduce the items before she moved them again, Jenny looked to see what was there. As she lifted one of the books, her eyes fell on the shoebox, and a wave of emotion engulfed her. Knowing what was inside, she hesitated, not sure if she could bear to see it again. Then taking a deep breath, she slowly lifted the lid. The letter was lying on top where she had placed it long ago. She held the yellowed pages carefully in her hands, frozen in time as she read it and recalled what happened. Her eyes stopped at the end of the letter and fixed on the signature—Jonathan.

The old hurt and helplessness of that day returned, and her tears welled up and spilled onto the pages. Finally, she wiped her eyes and put the letter back. In the days ahead she read it again...several times, always accompanied with the lingering afterthought—*I wonder how my life might have been.*

∾∾∾

Now Jenny was on her way to Europe and an eight-day vacation in Italy. When she first planned her trip, she discovered the route through Newark was little difference in price than a direct flight to Rome. She could not contain her excitement when she sat across the desk from the travel agent. Impulsively, she threw up both of her hands, clasping them together gleefully. "Wonderful! I have a good friend in Newark. Will I have time to see her at the airport?"

"Sure," the agent said, "you have a three and a half-hour lay-over."

After making travel arrangements, Jenny coordinated the rest—passport, packing, schedule changes, and so on. She made plans for a neighbor to pick up her mail, periodically check her house, and, of course, feed Willoughby the cat. Then, she telephoned Sandra. They would meet at the airport for lunch.

Jenny and Sandra were joined at the hip throughout their school years. They spent numerous nights together at one another's home. Those were usually Friday evenings when they could talk late into the night. Always, it would be after midnight before their final sleepy words. They spoke of boys, friends, fun experiences, and common dreams. Their plans were to go to college, then marry, have a family, and live near one another. The latter never happened. After college, Sandra married a man from New Jersey and headed east. Then the years passed.

※※※

The whirring sound of the plane's descent caught Jenny's attention and brought her back to the present. In a short time she would be talking with Sandra. She had never told her closest friend about her feelings for Jonathan. *Maybe this time…if the occasion is right.*

Jenny's heart raced as she departed the plane and entered the terminal. She looked out into the considerable crowd gathered to meet arriving passengers. A quick scan brought the realization she wouldn't need a nametag today. There was Sandra near the front of the throng, looking right at her, jumping up and down, waving.

After the hugs were exhausted, the two made their way to the nearest eating place; both knew the food didn't matter. They wanted to quickly find a private spot, and do what they loved most—talk. Fortunately, they found a booth in the corner and placed their orders, directing the waiter's attention to the first thing that caught their eye on the menu.

There was not much to catch up with, as far as major happenings in their lives. They had written and called each other through the years, accelerating their communication with the advent of email.

Relaxed, they looked at one another for a few seconds. *Has it really been twenty years?*

Jenny leaned forward. "Sandra, you really look good. Life has treated you well. Do you remember the things we wished when we were girls? It looks like it's all come true for you."

"Well," Sandra responded, "mostly it has." She discreetly phrased it that way, sensitive to her friend's past disappointments. Sandra knew Jenny had lost two husbands—one to divorce and the other to accidental death. The children she always wanted never materialized. By contrast, Sandra's life had, in the main, followed her script. She and her husband, Nik, had been married over thirty years. They had three grown children. Two of them were married, and one of them had given the family two grandchildren.

Sandra was determined to minimize the seemingly ideal path her life had taken, and said, "I don't think things ever turn out exactly the way we plan. At least, not for anyone I know. I'm grateful for my family, but families come with problems. You remember when I emailed you that our youngest, Clint, broke up with his fiancée? Now he has dropped out of college, lives with us, and works at a dead-end job. Nik and I are having difficulty dealing with that, so life isn't always pleasant around the house right now."

Sandra abruptly stopped and shifted the attention to her friend. "Jenny, I hated to hear about Jeff's accident." Pausing, she reached across the table, lightly gripping Jenny's hand. "I'm so sorry I wasn't there for you. I can't imagine losing my husband."

Jenny shook her head slowly, but said nothing.

JENNY KISSED ME!

"I understand if you don't want to talk about it," Sandra said softly, noticing her friend's hesitancy.

Jenny frowned and said, "It's not that, Sandra."

Seeing the pain in her face, Sandra responded. "What is it?"

Jenny looked down, unable to maintain eye contact as she spoke. "I didn't even cry at his funeral. There was no sorrow."

Sensing more words to come, Sandra didn't respond.

"I've kept it secret all these years, but I can't now… not with you." She raised her eyebrows. "Maybe it's time to unload."

Sandra nodded.

"For too long, I wore a mask. Our marriage was never good. The last couple of years were…unbearable for me. Jeff brought a lot of baggage to our marriage. His life was…so…so…messed up…." Jenny shook her head. "I'm sorry, I just can't talk about specifics." She took a deep breath and continued, "I kept up appearances when I communicated with you, because I couldn't face the humiliation of admitting another failed relationship. And I was weighed down with guilt, because I couldn't help him or save our marriage."

Sandra sighed as Jenny spoke.

"I know others saw me full of confidence during those high school and college years. It wasn't a façade. It was genuine. I really believed I could be successful at whatever I did. I don't know whether the success I had during those years bred my self-assurance or vice versa, but I can't recall failing at anything I really wanted…until these marriages." Jenny took a deep breath and exhaled. "I guess you could say...when I finally blew it, I did it in grand style."

"Jenny, you can't put all the blame on yourself. You're like a sister to me. You're the easiest person in the world to love. You've just been unlucky."

"No, Sandra, you want to make me feel good, and I love you for it. But I can't let myself off that easily. I've done a lot of painful soul-searching. The truth is...I was more unwise than unfortunate. In both cases, I married for the wrong reasons."

Sandra reacted with surprise. "You mean you didn't love them?"

"No, I don't mean that. I was in love...more so with Teller. That wasn't it. But I've had to examine the reasons I fell in love. There were character flaws in both of them from the very beginning of the relationships." She raised her eyes. "I chose to be blind to them."

She looked directly at Sandra. "You knew Tel. He was handsome, charming, articulate, smart, witty, and," she paused for emphasis, "selfish to the core."

Then, becoming aware of people at a nearby table, Jenny softened her tone and went on. "Tel worshipped success. That was his single, all-consuming focus. I know that's why he pursued me. I was pretty and gregarious—a nice trophy. I could help him reach his goal." She looked directly at Sandra. "He didn't develop that obsession *after* we married. He brought it down the aisle with him."

Jenny continued. "For several years before his affairs ended our marriage, the superficial qualities that first attracted me took on an ugliness. They became repugnant, because I'd foolishly fallen for them."

Her painful look intensified. "I faced what he really was before we married...but by then it was too late."

"Too late? What do you mean, Jenny?"

"I...I can't...I can't talk about that..." The hurt welled up inside of her again and she turned away. Thoughts of the shoebox returned.

She reached for her glass, took a sip, and said, "Sandra, I'm embarrassed about dumping all this on you." Then for the first time since Jenny bared her soul, she managed a smile. "Some friend, huh?"

Sandra smiled. "No Jenny, I'd do the same with you."

"I know you would. I hope it doesn't sound like I'm bitter. I can't say it's totally disappeared, but it's better, much better. I believe in forgiveness. It's the right thing. All of us need it. If we fail to forgive, it only brings misery into our own life."

"I know."

Squeezing her friend's hand, Jenny said, "I've wanted to share this with you for a long time. Thanks for listening. You are still my best friend ever."

"Would you like anything else"? They looked up to see the waiter standing at their table. Both smiled as they looked at their plates. There were not more than a half dozen bites taken between them.

"You can take the plates, thank you. And no, I don't believe we want...well, just a minute." Sandra looked at Jenny. "Do you still drink coffee?"

"No, I inhale it." Jenny said with a smile. "I'd love some, and by the way, Sandra, I'm picking up the tab."

"No you're not. I'm hosting. I live here."

"I don't care, this is my treat. Humor me," Jenny insisted. "If you don't, I'll remind you of that date you once had with Jimmy Hines. Better yet, I'll email Nik about it."

"Jimmy Hines. You wouldn't!"

"I would!"

As the waiter set their coffee down, the conversation ceased momentarily. Afterwards, Sandra said, "Jenny, many of the traits that drew you to Teller were no different from what the rest of us looked for back then. What we found attractive in a guy, things that turned on our romantic juices, were some of the very things you mentioned about him."

"I guess that's true, but everybody didn't mess up like I did, certainly not twice. You didn't foul up, Sandra."

Desiring to lift her friend's spirits, Sandra said, "Jenny, there's still time. You look younger than most of us, and you've kept your slim trim figure. The right guy might be out there yet."

"Thanks for the compliments, but you can't be serious." Jenny frowned.

"I am serious. And by the way, I love your hair change from dark to light. You're one of the lucky ones who can go blond after the grey starts to come in."

"Sandra, I surely don't need romance at this stage in my life...I really don't." Jenny's tone was not convincing. She knew it, and quickly changed the subject.

"You know what I've done in the last six months? I'm dying to tell." Jenny's eyes lit up. "I have a new job…I've moved to a new town…and I've built a new house. And just to top-off this newness kick, I've got a new name."

"What? You mean you've gone back to your maiden name?"

"No, no. I've kept Jeff's name. I have a new first name. I don't go by Jenny anymore. Everyone in my new surroundings calls me by my middle name, so I am Elaine now. Remember?"

Sandra grinned. "I can hear your dad now, '*Jennifer Elaine Nichols*, you two girls get to sleep. It's two o'clock in the morning!'"

"More like three." Jenny laughed. "And speaking of the new, this is my first trip overseas. Financially I'm in good shape. I've taught school in Dallas for most of my married life, and both husbands were good providers, but neither of them cared anything about traveling. So now, I'm able to do some things I've wanted to do for a long time—like this trip. Sandra, you're participating in the first episode of 'The World Travels of Jenny Ames,'—excuse me, *Elaine* Ames."

Jenny's eyes sparkled. "We're less than a week from the millennium. Imagine, our generation is about to experience something that hasn't happened in a thousand years. Since I don't have family to observe it with, I'll celebrate with this trip. Is there any better place than Italy? It does sound romantic, doesn't it."

"See Jenny, you *are* interested." Sandra's smile tarried, accompanied by a twinkle in her eyes informing Jenny that some thought had settled in her friend's mind.

"Okay, what is it?"

"What is what?"

"What are you thinking, Sandra? It's been a long time since I've seen you, but not too long for me to forget that look. What's on your mind?"

"You won't believe what happened last night. I was excited about seeing you, and I couldn't sleep, so I went into the den to watch TV. Guess what old movie was on?"

"What?"

"Here is a hint. What was the most romantic movie our senior year?"

"*Psycho.*" Jenny blurted out.

Sandra burst into laughter. "That really was our senior year, wasn't it."

"Sure was. I didn't take a shower for a month."

"Well, that explains it."

"What?"

"The heavy perfume. Jenny, I've got to tell you there were times when it was pretty stifling."

They both laughed. It was like old times.

"Back to your question, the movie was *A Summer Place*."

"Jenny, do you remember we saw it together on a double date."

"You're right, I had a date with the starting quarterback, and you had a date with Jimmy Hines."

Sandra laughed. "Would you get off that."

"You know what?" Jenny appeared serious. "In retrospect, I might have been better off with Norman Bates than a Troy Donahue type."

Sandra giggled. Her friend was back to her fun self.

JENNY KISSED ME!

"I still want to tell you what I thought when I watched the movie, Jenny. *A Summer Place* really was a soaper."

"But not to us back then. Remember, we loved it."

"You're right. I have to admit I still get a kick out of seeing it, if only for nostalgic purposes."

"Me too."

"Anyway when it was over, I sat there thinking about all those romantic fantasies we talked about years ago. Anyway, I ended up trying to think of the most romantic moment of my life." Sandra looked at Jenny inquisitively. "Got one?"

"Yes," Jenny said instantly, "but you have to go first."

"Well, I never arrived at a special one. But I did come up with three possibilities, and I can tell you this, none of them happened in the last quarter of a century."

They both laughed.

"What about you, Jenny? All those boyfriends you had. There must have been some moment that tops all the rest?"

Jenny sipped her coffee. Recalling her thoughts on the plane, she realized the time had come. The occasion was right. She could finally tell Sandra her long hidden secret. Leaning forward she whispered, "It was a poem."

Her friend stared. "A poem?"

With twinkling eyes, Jenny exclaimed, "Oh Sandra, if only you could have been there. There was a boy in our class named Jonathan. He was tall, nice looking, brown hair, and pretty brown eyes. Do you remember him?"

13

Sandra looked attentively at her. "Jonathan...what was his last name?"

Jenny slowly shook her head. "I can't even remember his last name. It was an unusual one. I'm not sure I'd even know it if I heard it now. Years ago I tried to find my high school annual to check his picture and name, but I couldn't locate it. He never came to any class reunions, so I haven't seen him in forty years." She sighed. "But he gave me a moment I'll never forget."

Sandra's eyes widened. "You've got my full attention. The mystery surrounding his name only makes it that much more romantic. So get on with it, I want to hear about it."

"Well, a unique thing about Jonathan was he loved poetry. I can even remember he competed in a poetry reading contest in high school. And let's face it, Sandra, that wasn't the ginchiest thing you could do back then."

"Ginchiest. I haven't heard that word since Eisenhower was president."

"Just setting the mood. You know, taking us back in time. Cool, hip, groovy, Edd Kookie Burns, *77 Sunset Strip*. Now, may I go on?"

"Please do." The flow of the conversation took Sandra back, and she joined in. "By the way Jenny, I know who you're talking about. Know why? At times, I thought you had a thing for him. As I remember, you talked about him some. I didn't know him well, but I think I had a class or two with him." Sandra squeezed Jenny's hand. "Please tell me about it."

Jenny looked down at her coffee and sighed.

JENNY KISSED ME!

Sandra waited for her response. She could tell by her friend's expression that Jenny was about to reveal something very dear to her.

"I had an English class with him in the ninth grade. We were all supposed to pick a poem, practice it, and then read it to the class. Most of us selected silly ones, especially the boys. Not him. He selected a beautiful poem about love. Only he didn't read it. He'd memorized it and recited it straight from his heart."

Jenny continued, delighted to finally tell someone about Jonathan, "The best part is that he looked right at *me* when he said it. It was like I was the only one in the room. This probably sounds vain, but as he said the words it was as if the poem was his, and he'd written it for me. When he finished, honestly, it took all the will power I could muster to keep from crying."

Sandra looked at her with both amazement and disappointment. "Jenny, we had no secrets, you and I. Why didn't you ever tell me about something that touched you so much?"

"I don't know for sure. I think I believed it was one of those special moments, just between two people." With a note of certainty in her tone she added, "I believe that was part of the reason."

"I can understand that."

"But, it was more than that." Jenny paused and looked down. "I'd rather not talk about the other reasons."

"Jenny, tell me about the poem."

"I read it again and again back then. I know it by heart. This may sound silly, but lately I've found some consolation in it. It takes me back to a special moment, a time when the feelings were there."

"That's not silly at all. Memories can do wonders for us. It must have been moving. Tell me about it."

"The poem was about a man expressing his enduring love for a woman, a love he promises will last in spite of the effects of time on her physical beauty."

"And Jonathan was looking right at you?"

Jenny nodded. "Sandra, back then I knew boys wanted to be around me just because I was pretty. When I heard Jonathan recite that poem, it seemed like to him there was so much more."

"I can understand why you picked that memory."

"I have mixed feelings about it now, Sandra. It takes me back to a magical moment. But when I come back to the present…reality sets in. I've never really known the love expressed in that poem." Jenny's countenance changed as she stared down at the table. "Now it's too late."

Soon their time was over, and the two friends walked to the boarding area. A curious Sandra said, "Jenny, I'm still thinking about Jonathan…you never told him about the poem, and your feelings?"

Jenny shook her head. "That's another story." With a faraway look, she said pensively, "It haunts me."

֍֍֍

After making Jenny promise to call from Italy, Sandra was on her way to the parking lot, thinking about what a great three hours they had together. Then a wave of sadness came over her, prompted by Jenny's words, "…now it's too late."

JENNY KISSED ME!

When Sandra arrived at her car and got inside, her sadness lingered. *If anyone deserves to be loved, it's Jenny.* The gloom suddenly vanished. She did not know why, but she knew, absolutely knew, Jenny was wrong. It was not too late. Sandra's smile grew wider as the possibility she imagined blossomed in her mind, spurred on by a single word—*Italy*.

Thomas Allen

TWO

Souvenirs and Strangers

John was two hours into his flight to Rome. He sat with closed eyes reflecting on the words of a poem he had memorized many years ago. It was like opening the door and welcoming an old friend—one who had not visited in a long time. The poem had been such an integral part of his life from the moment he discovered it, the summer before his senior year in high school. It had remained with him deep into his college years, until he married Claire and then it went away.

Now, he marveled at it once again, even as he had so many times before, because the poem really happened—the name was even the same.

> *Jenny kissed me when we met,*
> *Jumping from the chair she sat in.*
> *Time, you thief! who love to get*

JENNY KISSED ME!

Sweets into your list, put that in.
Say I'm weary, Say I'm sad;
Say that health and wealth have missed me;
Say I'm growing old, but add—
        Jenny kissed me!

John leaned back in his seat and drifted into the past. It was 1957, the opening day of school in a new town, and he was Jonathan again.

※ ※ ※

John's trip began with an earlier flight from his home in Phoenix to Atlanta. His daughter, Harper, left the airport after her father boarded. She grabbed the keys from her purse and walked from the terminal toward the parking lot. Her quick steps and broad grin made it obvious she completed her mission. As she started the car and drove out of the parking lot, she reflected on the rollercoaster ride her dad's emotions had taken the last few weeks. Until she actually saw him boarding, she was far from sure he would go through with the trip.

After more than two years, it was still difficult for Harper to imagine her father, or Pop as she called him, entering an empty house. He and her mother Claire had shared so much more than a residence—they had shared a life. It was a union of heart and mind and soul. Then a cruel intruder severed the relationship they had known for more than thirty years. Six months after the diagnosis, her mom was dead. Harper knew the moment the family left the cemetery she had lost more than one parent. A part of her father died on that chilly November day in 1997.

As Harper moved her car onto the freeway, her thoughts turned to something that would have seemed unthinkable a year ago. *Pop needs to find someone to love. I wish he could marry again. He is still young.*

In the past few months it had occurred to her intermittently, as she saw the continuing toll that grief was exacting on her father. Of course, she would never express those feelings to him, but they were there just the same. Today they came again as she watched him walk to the boarding pass counter. Seeing him from a distance, she realized why a friend of hers recently commented on how handsome he was.

But her friend was right, her father was attractive, the product of both genes and discipline. The latter reflected itself in one of his numerous guidelines to the good life, which he frequently shared with his family—unsolicited or not. "Be a good steward of your body, you are fearfully and wonderfully made." In his case that included exercising in the university gym twice a week.

Harper had admired the pay-off as she witnessed her father's tall athletic form lithely make its way across the floor at the airport, looking years shy of fifty-seven. There was one concession to age, but it was an asset. Graying temples, coupled with a strong jawline and deep penetrating brown eyes, added to his already distinguished look.

She mused, "Wouldn't it be wonderful if he met someone in Italy?" She shrugged her shoulders and

JENNY KISSED ME!

smiled as she continued her drive home. "Well, it doesn't hurt to dream."

༄༄༄

John Kaelin was an English professor in the College of Liberal Arts at the local university. He taught courses in Medieval Literature, Selected Plays of Shakespeare, and English Romantic Poetry. The latter was his passion.

Harper pictured a scene from the past...

Her dad sat in his chair as usual with an ever present book. His love of literature was evidenced even in her name—Harper. Harper Lee won the Pulitzer Prize for *To Kill a Mockingbird*, one of her dad's favorites.

"You reading poetry again, Pop?"

He nodded.

"When did you first start doing that?"

"Sweetie, I can't remember when I didn't."

"Did your friends read it too?"

"No, just me, 'til I met your mother in college." He grinned. "Then there were two of us."

"Mom says you're a romantic. What does she mean?"

"You want a dictionary definition?" he asked in a disinterested tone.

"No, I want yours."

Her dad removed his reading glasses and looked attentively at her. "Harper, I've always been moved by beauty...in nature...in human virtues like heroism. Really, I think in all things. Let me read a few words from one of my favorite poems." His glasses returned to his face. "I think this may help." He flipped a few pages to find what he looked for, then read the words as he always read poetry, as if he had written it himself.

> "She walks in beauty like the night
> Of cloudless climes and starry skies;"

Her father pulled his glasses down over the bridge of his nose, peering across the room at her mother, who busily prepared the evening meal. Then, closing the book, his retentive powers, which were extraordinary in remembering lines of poetry, took over.

> "And all that's best of dark and bright
> Meets in her aspect and her eyes:
> Thus mellow'd to that tender light
> Which heaven to gaudy day denies."

He paused, and glanced at his daughter over the top of his rims, nodding in the direction of her mom. "Harper, do you think your mother is beautiful?" He raised his voice slightly when he asked the question, and Harper suspected he did it deliberately, so her mother would hear what he was about to say.

"Sure, I do."

"I think so too, but that's not the reason I married her. Now listen to the rest of the poem. It's called 'She Walks in Beauty' written by Lord Byron. You've heard of him."

"Am I your daughter?"

"Well here's the way the poet closes,

JENNY KISSED ME!

> And on that cheek, and o'er that brow
> So soft, so calm, yet eloquent,
> The smiles that win, the tints that glow,
> But tell of days in goodness spent.
> A mind at peace with all below,
> A heart whose love is innocent."

Her father reached for his coffee sitting on the table by him. Taking a sip, he said, "Do you understand, Harp?"

"I think so. She's not just pretty; she's also good."

"That's what makes a person truly beautiful—a beauty of the soul—qualities like love, compassion, forgiveness. That's why I married your mother." As he looked over at his wife, he smiled. "Did you know she forgave me even before we met?"

"That story will have to wait, or dinner will be cold." His attempt to be overheard obviously worked.

Her father smiled as he glanced at her mom and she glanced back. As Harper went from one to the other, she saw the expression in their eyes that was there so often, and she grew warm inside. Their love for each other made her feel loved too …

As Harper replayed the scene, tears fell. How she longed to see his frequent smile and hear his daily impromptu poetry reciting once again. They disappeared the day her mom died—as he sat there by her bed holding her hand.

It was initially Harper's idea for him to take an overseas trip. She first suggested it about a year after her mom's death. Harper and her husband Jerry lived close to her dad, and every day Harper called the university to check on him after his last class...

She dialed the phone and heard a weak, "Hello."

"Pop, Jerry's grilling burgers tonight. Why don't you join us?"

There was no response and for the first time since the funeral, she heard him cry. Harper waited. In a broken voice, her father related how he recited a poem in class and became overwhelmed with thoughts of her mom, so much so, it was impossible for him to go on. He had to excuse himself and leave the room. They talked about it awhile, and as the conversation was about to end, Harper spontaneously presented an idea she conceived earlier, hoping to bring her father some relief.

"I've got a great idea, Pop. Now, please hear me out before you answer." Harper spoke rapidly, determined to make her case before her father's expected rebuttal. "You have buried yourself in your work since mom died. I think you need a change. Why don't you take a trip? You and Mom always enjoyed traveling. You haven't gone anywhere recently; that's just not like you. Your semester break is about a month and a half away. You will be out of school for three weeks. It's a perfect time for a trip."

"Harper, I don't want to go anywhere, not without your mom. I'm not even going to think about it."

A few seconds later, aware of her good intentions, he said, "Well...maybe later I'll think about it."

In the year that followed, she mentioned it now and then with no success. Finally, one day as she picked up the phone Harper got what she wanted to hear, at least partially.

"Guess what, Harper? I'm going to take that trip you've been so subtly hounding me about." There was excitement in his voice. However, her buoyancy was short lived as he continued.

"You know what I've decided. I'm going to Italy."

Her father was quick to decipher the silence at the other end.

"I know what you're thinking, Harper. You believe I need to go some other place, somewhere your mother and I haven't been."

That is just what Harper thought. Her father needed to go somewhere to forget, not *Italy*. Her parents had gone overseas twice, first to England and Scotland, and then later to Italy for their twenty-fifth anniversary. They had returned bubbly. Italy had been perfect.

"Harper, my memories are all I have now. I want to go back and relive them."

Harper did not respond, but by the end of the week, she became more than reconciled to the idea. *It might be just what he needs. Maybe going back to experience their favorite time together can finally bring some closure.*

Before the departure date arrived, her dad's emotions vacillated. The deepest plunge took place the very night before his departure. He was reticent for most of the evening while Harper helped him pack. By the time he spoke the words, she was ready for them.

"Harp, I can't go through with this, not without—"

"You know Mom would want you to go," she pleaded. "She would insist on it."

Her dad sighed, shaking his head slowly. "I know. I know. It's just so hard."

"Pop, you can call me anytime, day or night."

She kissed his cheek and whispered in his ear, "For me, please."

He looked at his daughter. There were tears in her eyes. His thoughts flew back to that August evening 27 years ago, when he first held her in his arms. There were tears then too. He had looked at her face and those tiny hands, knowing they would always tug at his heartstrings.

He hugged her. "I'll keep in touch..."

෴෴෴

The flight from Phoenix—where John and Claire had lived and raised their two children—to Atlanta took about four hours. From there the next stop would be Rome. John took his seat next to the window over the wing. As the plane began its taxi to the runway, John glanced at the empty seat next to him. He was pleased, because he did not want to deal with a chatty neighbor. It was time for memories of Claire—souvenirs from the past. There were so many. Where would he begin? The answer came immediately, as his thoughts wandered back to the circumstances when they first met. Every time he returned to them, as he frequently had through the years, he would once again find amazement reflecting on one of life's little marvels—sometimes the best things come unexpectedly. Meeting Claire was one of those serendipitous moments—nearly missed by a botched blind date.

As years passed, he visited the occasion so often he could recall the dialogue with almost perfect precision. He mused, reveling in how reluctantly he participated in their first date. He would usually end the journey back in time by shaking his head in wonder. *There was almost a life without Claire.*

It happened their senior year in college. Two friends, Dan, a fraternity brother, and his fiancée, Ruby, concocted the blind date, determined to pair him with their idea of the perfect fit—another English Lit. major.

John chuckled as he reflected on his views about going out with a member of the opposite sex, sight unseen. He was hardly alone in his assessment that a blind date must, above all, pass the eyeball test. She had to be pretty, prettier, or prettiest—preferably the latter...

"I've been the blind date route before, Dan. I always end up looking at my watch more frequently than my date."

"Jonathan, this is—"

"Hold it Dan, let me finish. I even know where this conversation is headed. When I say, 'Is she good looking?' Ruby will reply, 'She has a great personality.' Then I'll phrase it a bit differently to make sure there's no miscommunication. 'Is she pretty?' And Ruby will enlighten me on how well she plays the piano and bakes brownies."

Undeterred, Dan began his sales pitch. "Jonathan, I know where you're coming from. I've been stung before, but this is different. Claire really is pretty and, incidentally, she does have a dynamite personality. I really don't know about the piano bit."

Jonathan looked at Ruby as she nodded in agreement. "All right," he said halfheartedly. "I'll do it. But if you're misleading me, the second time I look at my watch, I will announce I've come down with a terrible migraine, and you'll have to take me home. We are using your car, right Dan?"

"Yeah. Sure. I didn't know you had migraines."

"There's a first time for everything."

"This won't be the time. You'll see," Ruby said. "But you have to wait until weekend after next. Claire's busy this Friday and Saturday."

"Is she going to a Moose patrol meeting?"

Ruby frowned. "You're going to eat those words."

Their glowing endorsements had little impact on Jonathan's long-term memory. By the time the date night arrived, he had totally forgotten.

About nine-thirty that Friday evening, he was shooting a game of pool with a friend at the student center.

Dan burst upon the scene. "I saw your car outside. Do you know what night this is?"

Noticing the perturbed look on his friend's face and the agitation in his voice, Jonathan's eyes widened. He immediately got the message.

"Oh! No! I'm sorry. I blew it, didn't I."

"What do you think."

"Where is she?"

"She's at the dorm waiting. She *did* remember," he added sarcastically.

"Dan, I'll call and apologize and ask her out. Okay?"

"I guess it will have to be."

"I'll do it right now. Do you have her number?"

"Do I look like a telephone directory?" Dan scowled. "Ruby knows it. She's out in the car."

"Would you mind asking her for it? I don't imagine Ruby wants to see me."

"You're right-on about that. This makes you not only a scatterbrain, but a coward to boot. I'll spare you her wrath and get the number. But you owe me." He took a couple of steps toward the door and then spun around. "Do you also need a dime to make the call?" Though the words had a caustic ring, there was a grin at the end of them, the first one Jonathan saw since his buddy abruptly interrupted the game of eight-ball.

Moments later, Jonathan had Claire on the phone. After apologizing profusely, he begged for a second chance. She agreed to give him one.

The minute he hung up the phone, Jonathan knew he would not blunder again, nor would he need to mark the date on his calendar, because he looked forward to putting a face to such a lovely voice.

As it turned out, the waiting period was abbreviated. Quite by accident, he met her for the first time in the library, the night before their date. He was there to study for a test in *The History of the English Novel* and noticed a girl at a nearby table. He recognized her as someone in his class who sat on the opposite side of the room.

She was by herself at a table, with several books and notes scattered before her. On impulse, he walked over to ask a question about the test. He had never seen her up close and was immediately taken by her appearance. Claire was a pretty girl, not knockout pretty, but attractive. She was petite, with a blond spiral ponytail and large blue eyes. Still, the most salient physical trait capturing his attention when she looked up was her megawatt smile. It lit up their section of the library. He thought of Lord Byron. "…The smiles that win…."

"I'm sorry to bother you. I believe I'm studying for the same test you're studying for."

"You are. Your name is Jonathan, and you stood me up last Friday night." She spoke the words in a solemn tone and returned to her notes.

Stunned and speechless, time crept by as he tried to think of the perfect thing to say—there wasn't any. The faceless girl, he had uncomfortably envisioned waiting for him the week before, now had a face—and it was pretty. The verbal skills for which he was known failed him. Jonathan stood there, helplessly blank. After what seemed like an eternity, all that came out was an awkward, "You're Claire?"

Sensing his uneasiness, Claire came to his relief. She smiled and said, "Yes, I am. And you are forgiven. I just wanted to see you squirm for a minute—to make sure you're truly contrite."

"I am. Believe me. May I join you?"

"Will you promise not to talk loud? I don't want to be thrown out of the library." Looking down at her notes, she shook her head. "I don't know about you." However, this time she looked up quickly and he saw it again—the smile, wider than before.

It began that way. The date the next evening was great fun, but different. They went to the downtown theater to see a John Wayne western. Jonathan was a huge fan of The Duke, but this movie turned out to be quite forgettable—not because of the plot or acting, but because there was nothing to remember. Both of them were oblivious to what happened on the screen. They talked incessantly through the whole show, pausing only when the soundtrack for a big action scene distracted them and interrupted their quiet chatter.

Even though the evening flew by, the idea of asking Claire out again never occurred to him. There was another girl in his heart. Her name was Jenny. She had been there since his first year in high school.

Nevertheless, the following week launched what quickly became a routine—meeting every Tuesday and Thursday in the library to study. They located a secluded section where they could talk as well as read. As the semester moved on, the former became more frequent than the latter. They conversed about their families, friends, hometowns, and high school years. Most of all, the tie binding them was a love for the romantic poets. With Claire, he could talk about Byron, Keats, and Shelly. In a petite package of cuteness, wit, vibrancy, and intellect, he found another bona fide romantic.

One evening, Jonathan suggested the twice a week ritual encompass more of the campus.

"Would you like to go over to the student center and get a Coke?"

"No," she said emphatically, "but if you make it a Pepsi, I'd love to."

From that time on, the study nights were not complete without the trip. As the semester progressed, they were together more and more. Jonathan finally asked her for a second date.

"Claire, I've heard there's a romantic comedy showing at the downtown theater. It's called *Breakfast at Tiffany's*. Have you seen it?"

"No."

"Would you like to go?"

"Who's paying?"

The movie turned out to be an irresistible love story with an unforgettable ending. They were still talking about it, as they stood on the steps of her dormitory. Moved by the moment, John impulsively leaned over, and for the first time, kissed her. Then the words tumbled out. "Claire, I think I'm in love with you."

"What took you so long? I've known I was in love with you for at least three months, two days, six hours, and..." she glanced at her watch, "thirty-four minutes."

They decided to wait until after graduation to marry. Claire received her diploma in June while John finished in August. They planned a September wedding, knowing their passionate feelings would require a difficulty—withholding the consummation of their love for four long months. However, being the true romantics they were, they did wait, eagerly anticipating their wedding night.

Through the years, *Breakfast at Tiffany's* became one of their favorite late night movies. They never tired of watching it. One evening following a viewing, John learned of Claire's earlier deceit.

"I'll never forget the first time we saw it," John said.

JENNY KISSED ME!

"I'll never forget it either," Claire replied. "Vicki loved it as much as I did."

"What are you talking about?"

"You remember my roommate. I never told you, but the evening before I saw it with you I saw it with her."

"Then you deceived me."

"Not really, 'all's fair in love and war,' and if you remember, that same night I did confess I had been in love with you for quite some time." She pecked him on the cheek. "Didn't I?" Then she smiled that smile…

ଔଔଔ

The flight was smooth, and John's memory powers rewound to the wonderful days they spent together for their silver anniversary. How often during their trip to Italy, he or Claire, marveling at the history they experienced, would compare it to their own land…

On one occasion, Claire said it best. "My, this makes us realize how young our country is. We're still in the diaper stage."

It was ideal—two lovers touring romantic Italy. Memorable moments occurred daily. One of the most enchanting of all was in Florence. The evening sun was low as they stepped onto the Ponte Vecchio, the ancient bridge spanning the Arno River, constructed during Roman times.

When they got to the middle section and looked down the length of the river, John shared some of the romantic history of Florence with her—history he taught in one of his university classes.

"Claire, you know about Dante and Beatrice?"

"Only that it's one of the world's most famous love stories, but that's about it."

"Oh, yes, I remember, you managed to avoid Medieval Literature, didn't you. Courtly love, Arthurian romance, you missed out on some goodies."

"I also missed out on *Canterbury Tales*. I knew what I was doing."

"Well, if you really want to know about their love, I can give you the scoop, and I'll leave Chaucer out of it."

"It's a deal."

"Their love story happened right here in Florence."

She glanced at him from the corner of those blue eyes and said, "Share it with me. I'm all ears, and heart."

"The story unfolds like this. It is the late thirteenth century when Dante is nine and Beatrice is eight. They meet, and for him it is love at first sight, like Jacob and Rachel in the Bible. You remember the Genesis narrative. '…Jacob served seven years for Rachel; and they seemed unto him but a few days, for the love he had to her. '"

"Yes, I know the story." Then Claire added, "Would you have done that?"

"What?"

"Seven years, for me."

"Claire, let's stick to the subject. You're worse than some of my students."

"Well, go on then. This better be good."

"Dante becomes totally absorbed with Beatrice and seeks out locations hoping to spot her. However, it is

JENNY KISSED ME!

not until he is eighteen years old that she actually speaks to him. He approaches her walking down a street here in Florence. She is dressed in white and is in the company of two older women. Beatrice greets Dante and he is enthralled by the meeting. Later that evening, he has a dream that culminates in one of the world's greatest romantic poems, *La Vita Nuova*. Want to hear some of it, Claire?"

"You couldn't."

"I could, if my lover desires."

"Your lover awaits with bated breath."

"Then at your beck and call, my lady….

> She greeted me; and such was the virtue of her greeting that I seemed to experience the height of bliss. It was exactly the ninth hour of the day when she gave me her sweet greeting. As this was the first time she had ever spoken to me, I was filled with such joy, that, my senses reeling, I had to withdraw from the sight of others."

"Word for word, that's impressive." Claire tilted her head in approval.

"Well, the truth is I cheated. I knew we planned to see the Ponte Vecchio, so I memorized it for you. However, to quote someone from out of the past, 'all is fair in love and war.'" They laughed, kissing right there on the bridge.

"Claire…, I would."

"Would what?"

"Seven years…for you."

Swept up in the moment, oblivious to the small crowd around them, they gazed at one another totally captivated. Then they kissed again, as he held her in his arms...

On the plane now, in his mind's eye he saw Claire's face as he envisioned them leaving the bridge, walking hand in hand. It was as vivid as that day in Florence.

The aching returned. He missed her so.

ଏବଏବଏ

The flight from Atlanta overseas did not afford John the same solitude as the earlier one. This time he did have company—a stranger whose presence turned out to be quite eventful, launching memories of a long ago love, which occupied his mind for the remainder of the flight to Rome.

Sitting next to the window, John picked up one of the two books included in his carry-on when a middle-aged man plopped down on the seat next to him. John looked up, nodded in response to the man's "Hi!" and then lowered his sight once again to the literature he was reading. It was one of his *Harvard Classics*. He had grabbed it at home as he heard Harper honking to pick him up for the airport.

As much as he loved books, it was unusual he had not planned his reading material ahead of time for the flight. That was not normal for him; but this trip was not normal either. When Harper drove up, he was still debating within himself whether to go or not. The book he snatched was a book of poetry entitled *Collins to*

JENNY KISSED ME!

Fitzgerald, covering the period of the Romantics. The second book he brought with him—and soon regretted—was *The Four Loves,* by C. S. Lewis. Lewis, one of his favorite authors, was also a professor of Medieval Literature, prior to his death. John had placed the book on the pull down shelf in front of his seat.

A few minutes later the man who sat next to him leaned forward, looked at the book, and said, "C. S. Lewis, I've heard of him."

"Yes, he's quite well known."

"Didn't he write *The Chronicles of Narnia*?"

John covered his mouth to disguise a smile. For a split second, an antidote for unwanted conversation occurred to him. *If you sit next to someone you don't want to talk with on a plane, just ask him, 'Are you saved?' Chances are he will clam up immediately.* John resisted the impulse and responded curtly, "Yes he did write them."

"I read them as a kid. At the time, I didn't know they contained Christian symbolism. I found that out later."

"Yes, the *Chronicles* can be enjoyable even if you are unaware of the imagery."

Then the man pointed to the shelf. "That's interesting, what are the four loves?"

By now, realizing the end of this conversation was nowhere in the near future, John decided to relax and enjoy it. It simply was not in his nature to be rude.

"The four loves are affection, friendship…." Then he stopped and said, "Incidentally, each of them is based on a Greek word. Do you know the Greek word for friendship?"

"No." He shook his head.

"It's *Philia*. What is Philadelphia called?"

"The City of Brotherly Love," the man responded.

"There you have it," John said. "That's what the word means in Greek—fraternal love, the love of a friend or brother. You didn't think the city was called that because they treat people that way in Philadelphia, did you?"

The man chuckled.

Sensing the opportunity for a playful moment, John asked, "You're not from Philadelphia are you?"

"Not hardly, I live just outside of Atlanta."

"That figures, had you been from Philly, you would have come after me like I had on a Dallas Cowboys' jersey."

"I like your sense of humor." he said with a grin.

"Well it helps one get through life. Anyway, the other two loves are Eros and Agape, or divine love."

"Eros? As a Christian writer, I don't imagine Lewis had much use for that." Max paused. "I've read he was a misogynist, you know, he didn't like women."

"Far from it. He had a deep admiration for the opposite sex, and a number of women had a strong influence in his life."

Suddenly John found the dialogue intellectually stimulating. *Misogynist. This fellow must have read a book or two. You don't pick up a word like that down at the local sports bar.*

John extended his hand. "Before we continue, my name is John."

"I'm Max."

"Well Max, Eros has a place in Lewis' thoughts on love. Have you read the Song of Songs in the Old Testament?"

"No."

"If you do, you'll realize the Hebrew canon of scripture also has an appreciation for romantic love."

Max's eyes lit up. "Pretty explicit, huh?"

"Not by today's Hollywood standards, but the physical attraction the two lovers have for each other is very pronounced. How is this for an opening line in a book, Max?

> Let him kiss me with the kisses of his mouth:
> for thy love is better than wine."

With obvious surprise, Max said. "That's in the Bible?"

"It sure is. Are you bored yet?"

"Not the slightest." Max grinned. "It's a long flight to Rome."

"Good," John continued—warming to the teaching opportunity. "But Eros is different from just physical desire. Lewis describes it as 'that sense of being in love.' Well, here's the book, let me just read a little."

Within less than a minute, John found the excerpt he looked for.

"Listen to this Max, it's in the chapter on Eros.

> 'Very often what comes first is simply a delighted preoccupation with the Beloved—a general, unspecified preoccupation with her in her totality. A man in this state really hasn't leisure to think of sex. He is too busy thinking of a person....

If you ask him what he wanted, the true reply would often be, 'to go on thinking of her.'"

Max rubbed his chin with his index finger. "You know, I might want to read that book sometime."

John smiled. "Tell you what. If you want to read it, I'll give it to you. I have read it several times."

"You sure?" Max asked.

"Absolutely, happy to do it. I'm a teacher so I encourage reading. Frankly, I give away books all the time. While we're on the subject, in regard to that misogynist label, there is one more thing about Lewis. He was a bachelor for most of his life, but in his late fifties he married. He once confessed to a friend that he didn't expect to find in his sixties what he had missed in his twenties. The love Lewis found was Eros. He knew the woman for several years prior to their union. They first experienced friendship. Later, their *Philia* merged with *Eros*."

"You've piqued my interest. May I see it?"

"It's yours," John replied, handing it over to Max.

As Max opened the book, John informed his new acquaintance, "I think I'll get a little shut-eye before dinner."

"You deserve it. I made you work during your vacation. Thanks for the conversation and the book."

৯৯৯

John's comment was a bit misleading, for he knew sleep was not coming. It never did on plane trips. But the part about closed eyelids was accurate. He could hardly wait to welcome memories of long ago.

The passages he had read to Max—"*preoccupation with the beloved*" and "*to go on thinking of her*"—brought back thoughts of a girl and a poem. The words came back to him as if it were yesterday. "*Jenny kissed me when we met...*"

She had been his first love, his first encounter with Eros.

If Max had looked his way, he would have surely seen John's lips change into a smile as he immersed himself in the past. He was fourteen again, about to see Jenny for the first time.

THREE

Eros Descends

John (or Jonathan, as he now thought of himself) moved the back of his seat to an incline, leaned his head back and took a deep breath, realizing where this journey back in time would take him. He was about to resurrect a moment he had not thought about since his college days. The instant it happened he stored it in his memory chest, along with so many other Jenny moments, including the pinnacle one his senior year in high school—her kiss.

At the time, he had buried all of them deeply—for Jenny was a secret love, and only he had access to the memories. Through most of his high school days he had revisited them more times than he could count, but that was over forty years ago. Then he had closed the chest the evening he kissed Claire on the dormitory steps.

As excitement grew within him, a gleam spread across his face. *I'm not going to rush this.* He nodded slowly as he tendered the resolve. *I know the feeling—I'm going to remember Jenny...it's been a long, long, time. I want to enjoy the trip.*

Jonathan's thoughts drifted to a small town in central Texas. In the winter of 1956, during the Christmas holidays, he and his family moved to San Marcos following the unexpected death of his father. Jonathan was fourteen at the time. After finishing college, he left San Marcos to pursue a doctorate at a university in another state. Over the following decade, he always went home at Christmas—then after his mother's funeral in 1975 he never returned. He thought of the changes that took place from the time he moved there until 1975. Even then, it was somewhat different from the Jenny years. *It's been a quarter of a century since I've been home. I'm sure I probably wouldn't even recognize some places, but I do remember the way it was the first time I saw her...*

San Marcos, gateway to the Texas Hill Country, was a scenic town, and its attractiveness paid off commercially. One thing Jonathan noticed the first time he entered the city limits, in the back seat of a 1949 Ford, was a line of motels on the outskirts. Back in the 1950s, these roadside lodgings were a phenomenon common to large cities and tourist locales. San Marcos numbered among the latter. Its modest population of twelve thousand souls swelled during the summer tourist season with hordes of out-of-towners. Motels housed the influx, along with numerous summer cabins lining the San Marcos River.

The city's aesthetic and economic good fortune were credited to its location along the three hundred mile Balcones fault line. Though dormant now, it formed the Balcones escarpment, marking the boundary of the Texas Hill Country and the Coastal Plains. Springs of clear, sweet water surfaced all along the fault, including San Marcos Springs. It gave rise to the city's chief attraction, which brought tourists streaming into the area. Aquarena, as it was called, featured glass bottom boat rides, a sky ride, and a submarine theater with mermaid dancers performing underwater ballet. Jonathan smiled when he thought about the biggest crowd pleaser of all, Ralph the Swimming Pig. Ralph even made an appearance on national television.

The fault was also responsible for another lucrative tourist business. While forming the escarpment above, it produced caves below. One of these, dubbed Wonder Cave, was the oldest commercial cavern in the state. Jonathan worked there as a tour guide, the summer of his first romance.

It was not, however, the attractiveness of the town that prompted his mother to move the family. San Marcos was a college town, the home of Southwest Texas State Teacher's College, and she determined her three children would have a college education. Jonathan understood her foresight concerning their future schooling, but nonetheless, the move was emotionally devastating. Having spent all of his conscious life in one place, a town in east Texas, this relocation to unfamiliar surroundings only intensified the trauma which had begun on that early Sunday morning in October when his mother's scream woke him to the news of his father's death.

Within weeks of that event Jonathan perceived a change in his own personality. He was by nature outgoing, now he turned inward. It was as if a new person entered his body, one whose sole wish was simply to be left alone.

It was in this state of mind that he attended his first day of school in this new location, and he saw Jenny. Before that moment, he was aware of nothing but a mass of nameless faces moving, talking, and joking. They were indistinct and impersonal—completely detached from the self-imposed seclusion reigning within. He spoke to no one, acknowledged no one, smiled at no one. At his locker, when a student attempted to initiate a conversation, Jonathan's response was brusque. He did not want to be bothered, and he didn't mind who knew it. That first day the morning hours passed in snail-like fashion. Jonathan found himself glancing at his watch shortly after his first class began. *Will this day ever end?*

The lunch bell rang. He followed the other students to the cafeteria, bumping and maneuvering his way through the crowd. He walked through the cafeteria line unconscious of everyone around him. Then he carefully searched to find surroundings with the biggest gap between him and anyone else. He realized his quest when he spotted an empty table by the window. The first few minutes after he sat down, he didn't look up, limiting his focus to the bland food that lay before him. Periodically, he forced a few bites.

Then he heard a laugh. It was hardly the only laughter in the room. The chatter, teasing, and horseplay all around him produced an abundance of it. However, this laugh was different...

On the plane all these many decades later he still remembered it. *What was there about that laugh that caused me to look up, when I tried so hard to ignore the happenings around me? It was soft, sweet, absolutely infectious. Even if you missed the joke, or were not privy to the conversation, you still had to join in—it was that contagious...*

At the time, Jonathan did not join in, at least not outwardly. A slight grin appeared on his face, betraying the truth that there was still room for some laughter inside. When he could no longer resist, he looked up to identify the source of that alluring sound, and he saw her face.

Jenny sat at the table across from him. She was near enough that he saw beautiful deep-set dark eyes framed by the fairest complexion, long black hair—constantly in motion on the shoulders of her red sweater—and that captivating smile. For a full five minutes, she was the only person there, occupying his entire consciousness. His trance-like gaze made him oblivious to anyone or anything else in the room...

As John's mind now played back the scene, it settled on a similarity. He remembered he had been in love twice during his life, and in both instances an arresting smile attracted him. Though with Jenny, it was much more. The effect her image had on his senses was unlike anything he had ever experienced—at least in real life.

JENNY KISSED ME!

There was a comparable visage on the movie screen. Though he was only eleven at the time, he was old enough to experience the stunning effect of beauty in a member of the opposite sex. It was one of those rare instances in his childhood when his dad loaded up the family and took them to the drive-in theater. While the credits flashed, he and his older brother went to the concession stand to buy popcorn and soda pop. When they returned to the car, the story was already on the screen. Jonathan looked up and saw the face of a girl who sat in a tree. He was mesmerized. In the movie, her name was Sabrina. But the actress's name was Audrey Hepburn. He had never seen any face so beautiful.

Seeing Jenny the first time that day in the cafeteria had given him that same *Sabrina* feeling, only this time she was live. Seeing her at lunch that day was the beginning of his *Eros journey*. In one thrilling moment, Eros had descended and lifted him from a valley of despair to a peak of ecstasy. The experience was so overwhelming it would stay with him even beyond his high school years. Until Claire entered his life seven years later, rare was the day he never thought of Jenny.

ఴఴఴ

"Would you like something to drink?" The flight attendant's words startled him. They abruptly awakened his daydream, a dream he didn't want disturbed.

"No," he stammered.... "No thank you."

He returned to replaying that memory day…

As he went to classes after lunch, he continued to think about Jenny—always looking around, hoping to catch a glimpse of her. In English, his final class, what he wanted transpired. He arrived five minutes early. Then just seconds before the bell rang, Jenny entered the room.

Jonathan's eyes lit up. *I'll get to see her every afternoon.* Then, it dawned on him. *I don't even know who she is.... But no one that pretty can be around for long without her name being mentioned publicly.* Nevertheless, he was too impatient to rely on chance, even if it was dead certain.

He had to find out her name without revealing his feelings. Jenny sat in the second seat next to the door, which gave him an idea. Having plotted his strategy, it required him to do something he had not done all day. He would have to speak to someone. Oddly, that no longer bothered him, because after he saw Jenny in the cafeteria his perception of others changed. They seemed friendlier now, happier, and more likable. It was as if the beauty radiating from her face set aglow the world about him.

The moment the bell rang, Jonathan set his plan into action as he turned to the student behind him.

"Hey, my name's Jonathan. What's yours?"

"Rick."

A conversation ensued as they left the room and walked down the hall.

Determined to disguise his feelings, Jonathan asked casually, "I'm new here, trying to learn everyone's name. Do you know the names of the people who sit in the first three chairs next to the door?"

"Sure. The guy in the first chair is Bob. And the person you really want to know about is Jenny." As he slapped Jonathan on the back, Rick laughed. "Wherever you came from, you've got good eyesight."

Jonathan grinned. "Thanks Rick, see you tomorrow."

Three weeks later, Jonathan received an unexpected gift—the ideal way to get Jenny's attention. The gift bearer was Mrs. Bateman, the English teacher. Jonathan sat at his desk doodling, catching glimpses of Jenny out of the corner of his eye, when the good news was delivered. It was so perfect that he thought at first he must have imagined it, after all, he hadn't been paying the best of attention. But the gloomy look on the faces of the boys was a dead giveaway. He knew he hadn't misunderstood. Mrs. Bateman had indeed announced, "Everyone will be presenting poems before the class, beginning next week. You can choose any type of poem," she explained, "but it must be no less than a dozen lines. Tell me at least three days in advance the poem you plan to read and when you want to do it."

Jonathan could hardly contain his emotions. He knew immediately this assignment could capture Jenny's heart. Jonathan's love of poetry had begun during elementary school. He no longer recalled how, but early on it must have become obvious to his family, because one Christmas when he was in fifth grade an aunt gave him a copy of the *Best Loved Poems of the American People*. Although it contained a variety of categories, the initial one was his favorite—"Love and Friendship." Its contents encouraged a romantic propensity he seemed to have deeply embedded in his genes. When he opened it to the very first page, his eyes fell on the words.

> First time he kissed me, he but only kissed
> The fingers of this hand wherewith I write

The words were lines from *Sonnets from the Portuguese*, by Elizabeth Barrett Browning. Later he would discover that many considered her the best of England's poets, and some of the most famous opening lines in all of English literature would come from "Sonnet 43."

> How do I love thee, Let me count the ways.
> I love thee to the depth, and breath, and height.

He was hooked for life. Even back then, he knew one day he would be a teacher of poetry.

That afternoon, after English class, Jonathan's spirits soared. He knew he could have completed the assignment on the spot, drawing from his reservoir of memorized poems. Though the teacher's instructions were to *read* a poem, he already knew he would *recite* his. He would find the perfect poem to convey his feelings for Jenny and look right at her during his delivery. He could barely wait to get home, scan his poetry books and select the ideal one. At one thirty the next morning, he found it. He was ecstatic.

The next day Jonathan longed to tell Mrs. Bateman, "You can let me go first, I'm ready." However, after he thought it out, he rejected the idea. *No, I'll wait until we are almost through with the*

JENNY KISSED ME!

readings. My competitors for Jenny's hand will think this is sissy stuff. They'll probably choose topics about sports, or humor, or story poems. By the time it's my turn, this poetry-reading thing will be boring the entire class. Then, I'll make my presentation by memory and show 'em—especially Jenny.

At week's end, Jonathan shared his selection with Mrs. Bateman. She initially expressed surprise. He understood her response, because he knew no one else would choose that kind of poem.

"By the way, Mrs. Bateman, do you mind if I recite it from memory?"

"Well, of course not," she replied, "that will be just fine." As he turned to walk away, he heard the astonishment in her voice. "I am looking forward to it, Jonathan."

As the days past, he still had not actually met Jenny, so he started coming into class late. Just before the bell, he would walk in front of her and glance over to his left, ready to smile. When she was not talking with someone, which was rare, and happened to look his way, she too smiled. Then again, Jenny smiled at everyone.

Finally, the day to make his presentation arrived. Jonathan had spent many evenings in preparation. His selection had become a part of him—the poem's sentiments were his own.

The boy who preceded him predictably turned out to be the perfect contrast. Jonathan looked down at his desk, hiding a smile as he listened to a goofy rendition of "A Frog Went a Courting." It did get a response the student intended—class approval, evidenced in an

51

eruption of laughter. But that was not Jonathan's goal. What other students thought about his poem and how they reacted meant nothing to him. What Jenny thought and how she responded meant everything.

At last, Mrs. Bateman called his name.

Jonathan positioned himself to the left of the teacher's desk. That was the side of the room nearest Jenny. He planned to begin his poem without looking at her and then wait for the ideal moment when the words would have their most telling effect. At that moment, his eyes would meet Jenny's eyes—and she would know his heart.

Filled with emotion, which had been building since the day he saw her in the cafeteria, Jonathan began.

> "Believe me if all those endearing young charms,
> Which I gaze on so fondly to-day,
> Were to change by to-morrow,
> And fleet in my arms, like fairy-gifts fading away."

He paused, becoming aware of several boys near the back of the room smirking and giggling. Their actions only steeled his resolve and intensified his emotions.

> "Thou wouldst still be adored, as this moment thou art,
> Let thy loveliness fade as it will,
> And around the dear ruin, each wish of my heart.

JENNY KISSED ME!

Would entwine itself verdantly still."

Then—as rehearsed so many times before the mirror in his bedroom—he turned his eyes to the left. Only this time he was not visualizing her face on a blank wall, but gazing into the eyes of the one who had captured his heart five weeks before. He had never dared to look into those beautiful dark eyes. This time he dared.

Jonathan was center stage. This was his performance. And Jenny, who looked right at him, was his audience. Emotions swelling, he recited the finale,

> "It is not while beauty and youth are thine own,
> And thy cheeks unprofaned by a tear,
> That the fervor and faith of a soul may be known,
> To which time will but make thee more dear!
> No, the heart that has truly loved never forgets,
> But as truly loves on to the close,
> As the sunflower turns to her god when he sets
> The same look which she turned when he rose!"

When he finished, Jonathan's focus stayed on Jenny for a full five seconds, and then he glanced back toward the middle of the room. The smirks were gone. Some just stared at him, expressionless, as if they could not decide how to react to what they had seen and heard. A couple of guys looked down at their desktops. He also saw one girl with the scant trace of a tear running down her cheek. It was not Jenny. He didn't have the courage to look at her when he made his way back to his desk. Emotions spent, he dropped into his seat.

Mrs. Bateman rose from her chair. Always following a reading, she remained seated at her desk and would simply say, "Thank You." This time she had something more to say.

"Class, you have just heard a beautiful poem, recited as it was meant to be. Jonathan, your presentation was an inspiration."

Five minutes later, the bell rang and the class ended. As Jonathan gathered his books, three girls came over to congratulate him. Jenny was not among them.

Jonathan thanked them and then looked toward Jenny's desk near the door. She was not there either. *Surely, she's waiting in the hall*. A minute later, he realized it was wishful thinking. Jenny was nowhere in sight.

✥✥✥

At the dinner table that evening Jonathan hardly ate. His mother noticed and queried as to why. "I'm just not hungry," he responded. Then he excused himself and went quickly to his room.

He still couldn't believe what happened. Jenny left the class without saying one word to him. Negative thoughts rained down. *Boy, did I blow it.... I know what she thought. 'Who is this guy...and why is he looking at me?'* Most anguishing of all, he had emotionally exposed himself, not only to Jenny, but to the whole class. *I know what they thought too. 'Did you see who*

JENNY KISSED ME!

he stared at? How could he think Jenny would be interested in him?'

There was no escaping the truth. The perfect opportunity presented itself, and Jonathan's best effort failed. He knew the possibility of winning Jenny's heart had been squandered. *How dumb to think it could be otherwise.* Late that evening he found a slight reprieve. *At least it's Friday, maybe they'll forget about it by Monday.*

Before falling asleep, he reached a resolve. *This Jenny thing is over. She doesn't know I exist. So, as far as I'm concerned, neither does she.*

Monday, his resolution lasted most of the day. At noon in the cafeteria, Jonathan did not look at the table where she usually sat—even when he heard her laugh. He always looked at her during lunchtime as a warm-up for English class. Resisting the impulse, he was proud of his self-control. "This is not that hard," he told himself, taking a bite of what looked like left-over meatloaf. He shook his head. *They must have cooked this back when I recited that poem.* Tickled that he could now make light of it for the first time in three days, he managed a smile, mentally patting himself on the back as he spoke the words under his breath, "I'm over her." He continued to think that way until midway through English class, when he heard her name.

"Yes, Jenny?" Mrs. Bateman responded to her uplifted hand.

Jonathan instinctively glanced at her. And the feelings started again…

৵৵৵

55

Years later as an adult, John realized the movie, *Sabrina,* was more than his introduction to the hypnotic effect of beauty on the senses. It was also his initiation into the agony and ecstasy of unrequited love, a theme he later found so notably featured in poetry as well as song. He had experienced those ambivalent feelings many times during the Jenny years, along with a quality of Eros—She would not easily surrender the heart in which she had come to dwell.

John opened his eyes as he heard a passenger across the aisle stirring. He had been immersed in memories for over an hour, locked in the past. He glanced out the window of the plane. *I wonder where Jenny is now.*

FOUR

Haunted

The first thing Jenny noticed as she walked by the flight attendant and entered the Boeing 747 was its spaciousness. The sight brought immediate relief. Though she admitted it to no one, she suffered from claustrophobia. It was not severe, but it was uncomfortable. If she were alone, she would take the stairs rather than the elevator. As she got older, in typical Jenny fashion, she turned her liability into an asset by telling herself that she needed the exercise.

Now, as she made her way down the aisle and saw the passenger cabin was more than twice the size of a domestic airline, her fears took flight. She looked down at her purse and smiled. *I guess I won't need those anxiety pills after all.* She spotted her seat next to the window on the right and sat down, eager to reflect on her airport visit with Sandra.

The adage about old friends being the best friends was true. She realized how much she missed Sandra. She longed to see her more frequently, and had expressed that thought to her in their correspondence through the years. Before the two left the airport restaurant, Sandra had sprung a delightful surprise. "Jenny," she confided, "when Nik retires in five years, he's promised me this Texas girl's going back to her roots. He said it's my reward for being such a trooper." That good news called for a celebratory hug.

As she sat waiting for other passengers to board, Jenny wondered what Sandra thought about her recent changes—the new home, the new job, and especially the new name. Desiring to leave her friend on an upbeat note, she had enthusiastically interjected the theme of starting over again. However, Jenny had not talked about the details. At this stage in life, she was amazed how she had initiated so many changes in such a short period of time. Taking a job at a new school was the most difficult. She regretted leaving behind old friends—teacher associates she had known for decades. However, realizing the new school was within an hour of Dallas, friends would not be far away.

The name change was another matter. It happened impulsively, which was probably why Jenny was especially pleased with it. Her most memorable action in high school had been that way—impetuous—when she kissed Jonathan in the library. It had not mattered where she was or who saw it. It just happened. She left her chair to walk away, then suddenly returned to kiss him. The memory of that moment never ceased to thrill her.

Jenny was too sensible to allow spontaneity to rule her life altogether, but too adventurous to ban it completely. Choosing to leave behind the name she had worn for over five decades had not been part of any master plan...

When Jenny interviewed for her new teaching job in Denton, the principal looked up from reviewing her resume, and said, "Jennifer Elaine, which do you go by?" Before Jenny could answer, her inquirer added, "I love the name Elaine. That's my sister's name."

Jenny's response just popped out, "Elaine will be fine."

As she left the interview, Jenny reflected on her new name. In college she had encountered it in Arthurian legend while reading about the Knights of the Round Table. Elaine was the name of several notable women, the most famous had died of unrequited love for Lancelot. Given Jenny's romantic propensity, the discovery ushered in a sense of pride in her name. It became more than just a middle name, which her parents may have plucked out of mid-air.

As she returned to her car after being offered the job, she reveled in the serendipity. "From now on, I'm Elaine." She gleefully punctuated the announcement by tapping the horn in celebration as she pulled out of the parking lot...

Her overseas trip was similarly the product of a spur-of-the-moment decision. Four months earlier while driving home from school, Jenny listened to a Metroplex radio station which specialized in playing oldies. She heard the beautiful romantic song, "Al Di La" from the movie *Rome Adventure* being sung in

Italian. By the time she reached her driveway, she knew she was Italy bound. Two days later, she picked up the phone and made an appointment with a travel agent.

Thinking of Sandra again, she thought about her friend asking if she had ever told Jonathan about the poem. Jenny's failure to do so had haunted her since the discovery of the shoebox, five months ago. Now her thoughts returned to that special moment in the classroom...

After hearing Jonathan recite "Believe Me If All Those Endearing Young Charms," she stood outside the door to catch him as he left. But second thoughts changed her mind. *I wonder if anyone noticed he was looking at me. What would everyone think if I started talking to him? He's kind of different. The guys won't think he's cool.* Feeling uncomfortable with her thoughts she walked away. *Maybe I can tell him later.* But later didn't come to pass that year, or the next, or the year after...

The shoebox episode had prompted her to do some soul searching about why she had not told Jonathan that very first day when her emotions were the strongest. In retrospect, she knew the main reason was that she cared too much about what others thought. Appearances seemed to mean everything back then—how you dressed, the way you acted, but most of all who you ran around with—and Jenny was influenced by them.

In time, her desire to win favor with the right people became so obvious to her father that he brought the subject to her attention. It was late in her junior year. He had told her, "Jenny, if you trim yourself to suit all your friends, you'll soon whittle yourself away." Then he gently kissed her on the forehead. "Daughter, be genuine. There's a beautiful girl inside of you—just be yourself." When he walked away, he stopped and looked back. "Jenny, forget about what others think."

Yet, his message on authenticity did not fully dawn on her until one day in history class early in her senior year. Something the teacher said had triggered thoughts about an incident involving Jonathan that happened much earlier, but had been filed in her subconscious…

The teacher, Mrs. Laney, commented on the character of a certain Civil War general. "He *was* what he appeared to be." Jenny had instinctively looked over at Jonathan, who was busy taking notes. *That's Jonathan...he's real.*

Jenny's mind soon wandered. She left the scenes of Gettysburg, and Appomattox, for a scene in her bedroom three years earlier. She had just returned from a movie about Texas, called *Giant*. Its release had been anticipated as much as any movie Jenny could remember. It was appropriately named, because everything about it was humongous. It was set on a big ranch, in a big state, filled with big movie stars. Elizabeth Taylor and Rock Hudson made the movie on location in The Lone Star State. Then there was James Dean, who had charmed all the teenage girls, Jenny included, with his cinematic charisma. And they had mourned when his short life ended tragically at the age of twenty-four, in a car crash just after filming.

The film, in its larger-than-life Texas style, had an epic quality about it, but it also had something terribly disturbing to Jenny. It exposed—in vivid Technicolor for the entire nation to see—an ugliness about the state she loved so much. It depicted Mexican Americans treated as second-class citizens and victims of overt prejudice. Even though it was Hollywood produced and based on a novel with made-up characters, Jenny knew the fictionalized story was not mythical—she had first-hand evidence. Her hometown had a large Hispanic population, and the bias directed at them by the Anglo population was inescapable. Yet it had somehow evaded her consciousness until she saw the movie.

The most devastating blow was personal, because she recognized that she had no Hispanic friends even though she was constantly around them in school. She struggled to admit the painful reality that she did not look upon Latin Americans as her equals. Facing it was difficult, but in typical human fashion she eased the hurt by rationalizing, *but I'm no different from any of my friends. I'm just like them. None of them have—*

Her thoughts stopped. She knew that was not true, not completely. Jonathan did have Hispanic friends. She recalled something involving a Hispanic girl that had happened several months after Jonathan moved to San Marcos. Guadalupe was among a number of Latin American students from migrant farm worker families, who usually missed portions of the school year to work in other areas during harvest time. Jenny didn't even know her last name, but Jonathan did.

One day Mrs. Bateman, the English teacher, had looked up from her desk with a letter in her hand. "Jonathan, your name's on this. It came addressed to the school. Will you come get it?"

JENNY KISSED ME!

As Jonathan walked back to his seat, envelope in hand, Mrs. Bateman called out, "It's from Guadalupe. She may have intended it for the whole class. Will you check?"

You could have heard a pin drop as Jonathan sat down, opened it, and perused its contents. He looked up. "No, it's for me." Looking around, he added, "She's a friend."

Jenny was embarrassed for him from the moment Guadalupe's name was mentioned. She imagined the rest of the Anglos in the class experienced the same emotion. Yet, there was no uneasiness in Jonathan's voice. He had spoken the words strongly, matter-of-factly, and with clarity—"She's a friend."

The moment Jenny heard that last word, the feeling within her changed. Embarrassment vanished and some jealousy crept in. Not willing to acknowledge it, she quickly covered it with a barrage of diversions. *I wonder what was in the letter. Why did she write to him? Does he like her? This could hurt his reputation. Doesn't he care what others think?* Weeks later, Jenny's veiled suspicion about their relationship waned. She had noticed Jonathan's behavior during those intervening days, and a salient peculiarity set him apart from most Anglos—he had a number of Hispanic friends of both genders. But Jonathan's uniqueness had not fully dawned on her until she saw the movie, *Giant.*

Jenny's thoughts were interrupted when she heard classmates gathering their books. She glanced at her watch. There was five minutes left in the history class. Enough time to revisit the day Jonathan recited the poem to her. *He didn't care what others thought. He was just being himself.*

The third period bell rang, and the history class was over. Immediately Jenny's eyes were on Jonathan as he chatted with another student. The words came to her again. *"He was what he appeared to be…"*

As time passed, Jenny realized that the thoughts sparked in that high school history class her senior year, had not only deepened her attraction to Jonathan, but had influenced her life in a significant way. It was in evidence during the graduation ceremonies at the end of that school year. She sat next to Elena, a Hispanic girl. They had gone to school together since the third grade, but always at a distance. During Jenny's senior year their relationship changed, and Elena became a good friend. She was cheerful, witty, and smart as a tack—great fun to be around, and the recipient of Jenny's first hug after the ceremony.

Years later at one of her early class reunions, someone asked her which school year was her favorite, and she spontaneously responded, "Our senior year." And decades later, when she opened the shoebox, the answer was clear. She knew why—it was Jonathan. Her friendship with him blossomed that year, ending in a kiss, and that was reason enough…

That final year they had three classes together. In each one, she sat next to him. Though unknown to him, she had made sure of that. She found herself getting to class early and leaving late, so she could talk to him. They would often walk down the hall together after their classes.

JENNY KISSED ME!

Once her boyfriend asked her about Jonathan, and seemed to accept her explanation, "He's just a good friend, and he helps me in English."

She and Jonathan did talk about English class, but they also discussed much more. Jenny had never met anyone with such a variety of interests. Plus, there was always laughter. Jenny soon came to believe he was the funniest boy she had ever known. This increasing attraction to Jonathan led Jenny to a significant decision that year. She broke up with her boyfriend during the Christmas holidays. She convinced herself she was tired of the regimen of going steady and wanted to finish her senior year unattached. In truth, she knew better than that. Her true motivation was a hope that Jonathan would ask her out.

The spring term began, weeks became months, and there were no overtures from Jonathan. She wondered why. *We have fun in class. I know he likes me.* Then her thoughts would invariably go back to the regrets of that day when she first became aware of him. *Why didn't I tell him about the poem? What if he knew it kept me awake until three the next morning?* She was determined to show him how deep her own feelings were—deeper than feelings for any of the boys she had ever dated. She had done everything to get the message across to him, except honestly tell him.

One evening she almost did. She could vividly remember the scene as clearly as if it were yesterday. It was the night of the junior-senior prom. She had hoped Jonathan would ask her, but when he didn't, she agreed to go with an old boyfriend. During the course of the evening, her date excused himself to go to the restroom.

65

She had noticed him gesture for two other boys to join him, which meant he wanted to talk about whatever guys discuss on those occasions. She knew it would be a little while before he returned, so after he left her side, she looked around to see if she could spot Jonathan. He was there with a classmate she knew well. Jenny's glance was rewarded. He walked straight toward her.

"Jenny, I've never danced with you. This could be our last chance, and Pam said it's okay. What about it?"

"When I saw you coming over, I hoped you'd ask me."

"I couldn't resist. You look great in your red dress."

It took only a few minutes on the dance floor for Jenny to realize he was a very good dancer. It didn't surprise her. *Poets should be good dancers.*

As they moved around the floor, they talked.

"Are you going to the University of Texas next fall?" he said.

"Yes, it's close to home, so I can drive back here in less than an hour. Are you going to school here in San Marcos?"

"Uh huh, staying at home and saving a buck or two. I can't really afford to go out of town. But an advantage is I won't have to make all new friends. Several of us are going to be here at Southwest Texas."

The music ended. As he accompanied Jenny back, the familiar strains of the next song began. Jonathan stopped in his tracks. "Jenny, we've got to dance to this."

As they walked out to the dance floor, Jonathan said, "Did you know you were wearing red the first time I saw you?"

She didn't know what to say.

They danced in silence to their class song, the instrumental theme from *A Summer Place*. Immersed in the music as if they were part of it, Jenny wished that the song would go on forever. Now, in his arms, she had the strongest urge to empty her heart and share the feelings she had for him. This was the time and she knew it. "Jonathan," she began, but her heart started racing and the words just wouldn't come out. She could hardly breathe. "Jonathan, I'm going to miss you." That feeble attempt was the best she could do.

The dance ended, and she watched sadly as Jonathan walked away.

As far as Jenny was concerned, the dance that night was the final time they were together. Literally, it was not true. School still had another month to go, and they exchanged pleasantries in the hall, and chatted a bit in the classes they had together, but something had changed. Now their conversations were no different from any other classmate she happened to talk with. And the laughter was gone...

Years later, when she thought about those changes, she reasoned they had occurred because both she and Jonathan were aware they would soon go their separate ways. The sadness of their awareness seemed amplified by an inability on the part of either of them to say what was in their hearts...

Graduation day seemed to validate her theory. After the speeches and the receiving of diplomas came the obligatory congratulations among the graduates. About the time Jenny thought she had embraced everyone, she sensed someone looking at her. Jonathan stood about ten feet away. Their eyes met, and they walked toward one another. Then they hugged—just a bit longer than others. There was none of the "Congratulations!," or "I can't believe we did it!," or "We made it!"

After the embrace, they stepped back smiling as they looked at each other. Their smiles seemed more forced than real. It was clear to her that both of them wanted to say something, but couldn't. Then Jonathan turned and walked away. It was the last time she saw him...

FIVE

Jenny Moments

John glanced over at Max. The book he had given his traveling companion lay opened on his lap. Max was fast asleep. It would be awhile before the flight attendant served dinner, and then there would be the long night ahead. He imagined Max would spend a big portion of it in his current state, joining most passengers who seemed to melt into their seats at night on overseas flights. That would not be true of John. He had no desire for sleep as he eagerly anticipated releasing long suppressed thoughts of his first love—memories, so many memories.

As a romantic, the vows he had taken with Claire, "…and keep yourself only unto her, until death do you part," encompassed his whole being—heart, mind…even memories.

Now free to think of another, he yearned to softly speak her name out loud. "Jenny." He smiled as two words entered his consciousness—*Jenny Moments*. He had coined the expression his junior year when he wrote those two words on the front cover of a spiral notebook, and began writing the memories of those glorious encounters with Jenny that made him feel so alive. When they occurred, the mighty descent of Eros into his psyche launched his emotions into the stratosphere.

The initial entry recalled that Tuesday when she first spoke his name following his poem recitation…

As he entered the room, he heard, "Hi Jonathan!"

It overwhelmed him; all he could say was an awkward, "Oh…Hi."

He intended to say her name out loud, but it didn't come out. As soon as he arrived at his desk the berating began. *What an idiot! One day I recite a love poem to her, and now I act like I don't even know her name.* Determined not to botch it the next time, he thought of possible solutions. *Maybe I should come into the room and speak first, before I hear her voice.* A chill went through his soul. *But what if Jenny looks at me before I say anything, and I see those eyes…that smile…I'll freeze again…I know it. I won't even get out an "Oh…Hi."*

A remedy quickly dawned on him. Confidence surged as he considered his move. *I'll enter the classroom, look straight ahead, say her name, and then glance at her. I don't see how I could mess that up.* His optimism faded as quickly as it formed. *I'll probably*

JENNY KISSED ME!

trip and fall on my face. He frowned. *I th*\
keep my eyes on my feet.

The next afternoon arrived. He entered and then he spoke her name publicly for the first time. "Hi Jenny." His eyes bounced off of her. *I did it.*

"Hi Jonathan."

Instead of stumbling, he floated to his desk.

※※※

For Jonathan, high school revolved around Jenny's presence. His being in class with her determined his outlook for the coming year. The first day of each school year was mingled with excitement and apprehension. He would get few hours of sleep the night before. So much was riding on the singular question, *Will Jenny be in my history, science, algebra, or English class?* He longed to be near her.

His sophomore year, he entered each classroom with a purpose. *If she is in class, I'll go over and sit next to her.* The year was a mixed bag. She was in two of his classes, but in the first one he failed to find a place near her. Prior to the second as he watched four football players surround her desk, laughing and joking, the all too obvious revelation struck him. *You dummy, did you think you're the only one who wants to sit near the most beautiful girl in school?*

At year's end, Jonathan rated it a seven—plus or minus.

His junior year was better. Though he only had one class with her, they sat right next to each other. He was especially pleased, because it was a result of his foresight. That year Jonathan took an elective and made sure Jenny was the sole factor in his selection process. One day several weeks before the end of their sophomore year, he was walking behind Jenny and her friend Sandra as they made their way to the parking lot. Fortune smiled on him when Sandra suddenly stopped and headed back to the building. Jonathan acted quickly, moving briskly up to Jenny's side.

"Hey Jenny!"

"Hi Jonathan."

"Jenny, I've been thinking about what elective to take next year—speech, art, typing—what do you think?"

"Take typing. I know you're going to college, smart as you are. Typing will come in handy. I'm going to be in the class, so we can take it together."

Almost four months later, Jonathan sat in class at a typewriter, and next to him was Jenny—exactly as she said. As the bell rang, he gazed about the room. Only one other boy was in the class. Jonathan beamed and whispered under his breath, "Nicely done."

Jonathan struck gold his senior year. He not only had three classes with Jenny, but he sat next to her in each one of them. It was the year they became close friends. Again, his good fortune was no coincidence but the fruit of a careful plan. Jonathan arrived at each room immediately after the end of the previous class. He stationed himself outside the door and then, if Jenny showed up, he greeted her and walked with her to her desk where he would sit next to her.

It worked flawlessly in the first two classes, but in the third something unexpected threatened his plan.

JENNY KISSED ME!

They walked into the room talking with one another, while Jonathan marveled at how perfectly the day had gone. Then someone at the back of the room shouted Jenny's name, and she stopped to respond. Jonathan started to stop too, but realizing it would have exposed his intentions, he continued alone to an unoccupied desk on the last row near the windows. Disappointed, he looked down at his book. A few minutes later, when he heard the sound of a desk move, he looked across the aisle to see Jenny's smiling face. A quick glance about the room informed Jonathan she had walked past several empty desks—including one across from the most popular guy in school—to occupy the place next to him. He was ecstatic. *I get to sit next to Jenny in three classes this year.* He turned away from her to avoid revealing the beam on his face. *I think I hit the jackpot.*

One of those classes was second year typing, and this time Jonathan was the *only* boy in the class. Physics met across the hall at the same hour. Gender speaking, it had a very opposite makeup compared to Typing II. Most of the students were boys, and several of them were Jonathan's buddies. As he left typing that first day, the taunts came. "Jonathan, what's the problem? Was the Homemaking class already filled?"

Knowing he was not about to endure that all year, he took action. As soon as school was out, Jonathan headed to the library for a quick study and grabbed the first physics book he found. The next day when the jeering started, he responded with a playful cut of his own. "Next year in college when you need a term paper typed, just try reciting the second law of

73

thermodynamics…for all the good it'll do you." His retort did the trick. The teasing subsided. In the end, Jonathan felt quite comfortable with the arrangement—they had Pascal, but he had Jenny. He could live with that. He wished he could tell his buddies the real reason he took typing classes, but he kept the motive to himself. Jonathan's love for Jenny remained his secret.

ಲಾಲಾಲ

The impetus for the phrase "Jenny Moments" had happened early in his junior year. It confirmed the good news that she had *at least* taken notice of the poem he recited to her in the ninth grade.

Following his embarrassment that year, he had buried his talent. *I love poetry and I'll continue reading it—privately. But it's not cool with the in-crowd. The guys hate it, some girls love it, but the one girl I want to love it doesn't. What's the use.* For two years Jonathan's fondness for poetry remained private.

An Advanced Speech course brought it out of hiding. The class furnished most of the participants for the year's district debate competition, extemporaneous speech, poetry reading, and other verbal contests. About a month before the event, the speech teacher approached him.

"Jonathan, Mrs. Bateman told me you have quite a knack for poetry."

"I'm alright, I guess," Jonathan said, hoping to avoid a conversation.

"That's not what she told me. She said you're gifted—the best she's ever heard."

"She's just being nice."

JENNY KISSED ME!

"Well, we can find out if she's exaggerating. We want you to be our poetry reader in the district competition."

"Mr. Franklin," Jonathan pleaded, "I'd rather debate."

"We have our debate team, Jonathan. You're an okay debater, but not the best. Apparently you *are* the best at playing Walt Whitman. I need you to read poetry for me." He put his hand on Jonathan's shoulder. "Come on, do it for ol' San Marcos High."

So Jonathan was compelled to publically resurrect his talent once more—unless he could find a way out.

He immediately sought an escape, as he walked away from the teacher. *I'll get the flu.* The idea began to grow. *It's even the right time of year.* He frowned. *No. It's not gonna work. Mr. Franklin knows I don't want to do this. He'll be big-time suspicious. I have to come up with something else.* On the way to his next class he pondered the dilemma. *Only the judges will be in the room. Jenny won't be there to impress, even if I could.* Given his experience with poetry, he knew there was a strong possibility he could take home the top prize. He could imagine the morning intercom announcement. "*Congratulations to Jonathan Kaelin on winning first place in district poetry reading.*" The digs from his buddies would surely come—good-natured, but something he could live without. He arrived at the only plausible solution. *The way out of this is to deliberately lay an egg. Then none of the guys will know.*

He received his poem weeks in advance, but ignored it except for a cursory reading on contest day, while he walked to the room where poems were judged. About a dozen contestants sat around the room, and all but two preceded him. With the exception of one student, he was unimpressed. Finally, Jonathan heard his name called and he strolled to the front of the room. His opening words were monotone and stilted. However, as he continued, the words connected with his feelings, and he immersed himself more and more in the lyrics. He just could not recite it half-heartedly. He ended up winning second place. Those first three or four verses into the poem probably cost him the top prize.

On the way home, he covered his face with his hands as reality struck. *Great! There'll be an announcement Monday morning after all, and I can hear the jeers. "Good job Kaelin. You read some poetry, and ended up with a lousy second place?"*

ನಿನಿನಿ

Jenny was among those who listened to the announcements on Monday. She did not laugh. After school, as Jonathan left, he heard a voice behind call his name.

He immediately stopped. There was no mistaking who it was.

Catching up to him, Jenny said. "Congratulations on your poetry reading."

"Thanks, Jenny."

'

JENNY KISSED ME!

"You should have won first place. I've heard you recite poetry. I remember when you recited that poem in the ninth grade..." Her eyes fixed on him for a second. "Well, I have to run...cheerleader practice. I just had to tell you."

Jonathan watched Jenny hurry away. *She did remember.*

Suddenly she turned around. Her speech was soft, but strong enough to carry the distance that separated them. "Jonathan, you know tomorrow we're having class pictures made. I'd like one of you."

"I'd like one of you too, Jenny."

Jonathan revisited their conversation that evening with mixed emotions. *What did Jenny call it—a poem?* He wanted to blurt out, *it wasn't just a poem, Jenny. It was a poem for you. It was about you...and to you.* He decided she probably didn't even remember the sentiment. But he consoled himself. *At least she was impressed with my poetry reading. Maybe that day wasn't a complete flop after all.* His spirits rose. *She does want my picture.* Then they rose even higher. *And I'll have a picture of her.* Now the horizon of opportunities to see Jenny's face had suddenly broadened. They would no longer be limited to the school hours. That last contemplation soared this Jenny Moment to the top of his list. It was the best ever!

Weeks later when everyone exchanged pictures, Jonathan was certain that Jenny must have included his as one among many. His photograph of her, of course, received special treatment. He selected a small frame at the drugstore and carefully centered her picture in it. He placed it on his desk in his bedroom. Of course, it quickly disappeared into the drawer when any of his friends came over. No one could ever know…

༺༻

John glanced out the window of the plane. It was solid blue with clouds below. He gazed at his watch. What he saw pleased him—five more hours to think about Jenny. So his eyes closed again, as he reflected on his high school resolve to let no one know his feelings for her. *There was that one time—Oliver. He found me out.* John chuckled. *I had one fight in my life, and it was about Jenny.* He shook his head slowly and smiled as an episode from the past flashed before him, one which had compelled him to make public a talent other than his poetry reading. He had been good at boxing…

When the incident occurred, it didn't merit an intercom announcement from the vice principal, but it did result in a visit to his office. Though known only to a few, Jonathan had become quite adept at boxing, because of his friendship with Ben, a Hispanic classmate. One of the first students that went out of his way to make friends with Jonathan during his early weeks in school was Ben. One day their junior year, Jonathan found out Ben had boxed in the Golden Gloves. It immediately captured his attention, and Ben took note. He invited Jonathan to come down to a gym in the Latino part of town and meet the man who mentored him. From then on, Thursday evenings became synonymous with boxing gloves, shorts, tennis shoes, and the smell of sweat.

JENNY KISSED ME!

Jonathan did not limit his training to the gym. When there was no one around to box, he practiced in other ways—skipping rope, shadow boxing, even throwing punches at his bedroom mirror. He also read a book, *The Pugilistic Art*. Later, in the spring of the year, his training paid off—in defense of Jenny.

One day after biology class Jonathan spotted Jenny as she walked down the hall toward him. She was talking with two other classmates and didn't notice him. His eyes, as usual, were trained on her.

Oliver Quirt, standing next to him, noticed Jonathan's preoccupation. Oliver was one of the few people in school that Jonathan totally disliked—and he was not the only one who thought that way.

Oliver elbowed him in the ribs. "I sure would like to make her."

Roused from his fixation with Jenny, Jonathan's eyes narrowed and shot a hard glance at the intruder. "What?"

Oliver stepped in front of Jonathan. "You know what I mean...Jenny...you'd like to do it too," he leered.

Jonathan felt his jaw and his fists clench simultaneously. His face burned red, angered by the remarks, and he let fly with a hard left jab on target to the spot where Oliver's smirk lingered. The impact of the blow, coupled with Oliver's backward reaction to neutralize it, dumped him flat on his back.

Jonathan's adversary rose quickly to his feet and headed for his assailant. Standing his ground, Jonathan slowed his opponent's advance with a left feint. Then shifting his weight to his right side, he stepped into another blow, tagging Oliver's jaw with all the force his right hand could muster. Oliver dropped like a rock.

Dazed and wobbly, Oliver got up slowly. With blood dripping on his shirt as he rose to his knees, he stared befuddled at the person looming over him. Although in a state of confusion, he was lucid enough to know the fight was over.

Unfortunately for Jonathan, the site of the fracas made detection by the powers that be virtually certain. It was outside a classroom adjacent to the vice principal's office. When Jonathan's fist landed squarely on the side of Oliver's face, the sound could be heard a hundred feet down the hall. Mr. Herrick's office was less than thirty and his door was open.

The blow, coupled with the crowd's gleeful shout "*Fight!*" brought the vice principal running. Jonathan's attempt to slip away into the mass of students was abruptly halted by a firm hand that gripped his shoulder. Mr. Herrick spoke sternly, "You and Oliver come with me." Seating the two combatants a safe distance apart in his office, Mr. Herrick turned toward the door and said in a brusque voice, "I'll be back in a minute to deal with you two."

Jonathan assumed the ploy was psychological—*He wants us to sweat a little, put a scare into us.* If that were the case, it would not work with Jonathan, who considered what he did fully justified. It was for Jenny's sake. Whatever the punishment, even expulsion, he could endure it. Besides, he figured he was in much better shape than the other fellow. Without turning his head, Jonathan caught a glimpse of Oliver— holding a bloody handkerchief over his mouth.

JENNY KISSED ME!

A habitual troublemaker, Oliver had surely been in this room many times before. Jonathan, by contrast, had a clean rap sheet. He had never been to the principal's office, at least not in San Marcos. *I haven't been in this situation since sixth grade in Baytown.* While he waited, he entertained himself by remembering what brought it about. It was the result of a mischievous streak he sometimes found difficult to contain. It happened in a classroom…

Jonathan had sat at his desk while his best friend worked a math problem at the chalkboard. The temptation was too much to resist. Breaking off part of a large paperclip and securing a rubber band for the launching mechanism, he pulled it back as far as he dared, and let it fly at his buddy's backside. It was a direct hit between the shoulder blades, confirmed by his friend's loud shriek.

"Alright who did that?" an angry Miss Denault demanded.

Influenced by the story of George Washington and the cherry tree, which, whether true or not, was an integral part of the lore of the day, Jonathan raised his hand and confessed, "I cannot tell a lie." Dangling the rubber band from his thumb he added, "*This* is the culprit." The class laughed. Miss Denault didn't. Jonathan was sent to the principal's office…

Jonathan's smile disappeared as Mr. Herrick's abrupt return brought Jonathan's focus back to the present situation. The inquisition was brief. Jonathan suspected that Oliver's bleeding lip, which had not stopped, was a factor. After a reprimand, warning, and a demand for the obligatory hand shake between the two combatants, Mr. Herrick dismissed Oliver with the words, "Go see Nurse Haley. You may need stitches. And Oliver, I don't want to see you in here again."

"Jonathan," he added, "I have more to say to you."

After Oliver's exit, Mr. Herrick put his arm around Jonathan's shoulders. "I'm surprised at you...not at him, but at you. And disappointed."

"I'm sorry, Mr. Herrick. We had some words and I lost control. It won't happen again."

As Jonathan started to leave, Mr. Herrick's words halted him. "Jonathan, I thought poetry readers were lovers, not fighters." He patted Jonathan's shoulder. "You must've really clobbered him. But if you tell anyone I said that, I'll deny it and suspend you for three days. Now, get out of here!"

Hurrying down the hall, Jonathan rushed to catch the bleeding victim before he reached the door of the nurse's station. He shouted, "Oliver, wait!"

Oliver turned his head, and Jonathan motioned for him to come closer. Cautiously, Oliver slowly turned back and closed the distance between them, gazing at the floor to hide the fear in his eyes.

Jonathan spoke softly although his eyes flashed, "Oliver, you keep quiet about why I hit you. If you tell anybody, we're going at it again...away from school, and I'll finish the job. That's a promise. Oliver, look at me." He held up his fist to emphasize his words. "No more remarks about Jenny. She's off limits."

The next morning Jonathan's right hand was swollen to the size of a grapefruit. It had throbbed all night, but the pain was external. Inside, he felt great. He was Don Quixote, and Jenny was his Dulcinea. He had defended her honor. While attempting in vain to tighten his enlarged fist, he viewed it with admiration. *There's my jousting lance, marred but triumphant, proof of my love for Lady Jennifer.* He chuckled to himself. *Thanks, Oliver, you jerk.*

Fortunately, there would be no need to tell his friends why he and Oliver fought. If they pressed him for specifics, a terse answer would suffice. "Oliver was just being Oliver." So the secret was safe...

※※※

John looked up at the flight monitor in the front of the cabin. As the green line moved across the map toward their destination, his thoughts returned to other Jenny Moments. There was an even better one their final year in high school, when Jenny became aware of another dimension of his personality. Before then, Jenny didn't know Jonathan had a playful nature that led him to initiate more than his share of good times. Once Jenny became aware of it, it increased her attraction to him. And he received a response from her that he had never experienced before.

It happened early in his senior year. Jonathan took a part time job, after school and on weekends, at the Holiday Theater. Primarily he was a doorman, which meant he took the customer's ticket, tore it in two, and gave half back while he deposited the other stub in the ticket box. Occasionally, a customer would hand him a free pass, received from either the owner or the theater manager. Jonathan was supposed to return those for re-circulation.

Several months into the job, Jonathan decided friends of his were more in need of the free passes than prosperous businessmen who were the usual recipients. Consequently, rather than returning all of them, he held back a few to pass on to his buddies. That practice set the stage for "Buck's Bonanza." Through the years, whenever John thought about it, he'd laugh uproariously.

The arrival in town of a Hercules flick made the moment possible. In those days, several cheesy movies about the muscle man of Greek mythology made the theater rounds. One of them, *Hercules Unchained,* came around while Jonathan was scheduled to work…

Thursday, at the opening of the matinee, a classmate named Zach came in. He was a character, willing to do just about anything for a laugh. He had a habit of pulling up one of his shirt sleeves, flexing his well-developed bicep, and uttering a defiant, "You don't want to mess with that."

The idea arrived in a flash of inspiration. "Zach, you want to earn two free movie passes? I have them in my pocket."

"You name it, I'm ready."

"Jump up on the stage while the movie is going on…give'em some *live* Hercules—you know, the muscle flexing stuff…and the tickets are yours. You on?"

"What do you think."

Zach walked into the auditorium. Jonathan followed, propping the doors open to get a view while he kept an eye on the ticket box.

84

JENNY KISSED ME!

His classmate immediately walked down to the front, leaped onto the stage during the movie, and started his performance. Laughter erupted in the theater. The instigator joined in.

That night Jonathan left the theater about nine and headed straight for his friend Buck's house. He could not contain his exuberance. He burst into his friend's room. "Buck, I've got an idea that will turn Barnum and Bailey green with envy."

Buck was lying on his bed, skimming a copy of *National Geographic*, mainly stopping at the pictures. As his friend stood up, Jonathan beamed at the sight. Buck stood six foot four and weighed possibly 140 pounds—if he had both pockets stuffed with quarters. He could run through a shower without getting wet, if he zigged and sagged at the right moment. Buck was not his given name. Classmates knew him as Randle. Jonathan ran around with him for almost two years before he ever heard the nickname.

Randle's father enlightened him one evening when Jonathan was at their house.

"Buck, come in here. I want to talk to you about something."

Jonathan looked around and then back at Randle. "Who's he talking to?"

"Me," Randle replied, his face growing redder by the second. "He used to call me that when I was little. He knows I hate it."

"Then why does he do it...*Buck?*" Jonathan asked with an impish grin.

"To irritate me...just like you're doing."

From then on, it was Buck.

His scrawny friend would be perfect for an exhibition like the one Jonathan witnessed that afternoon. Only this would not be for a measly Thursday matinee. His sights were set on a much larger audience. This would be for the Saturday night show, when the high school crowd flocked to the local cinema. Buck was not only ideal for the part, he was also willing even before Jonathan asked.

"Buck, you know what Zach did this afternoon?"

"No, but I think I'm about to find out."

"You are. The theater is showing one of those Hercules movies. Today, Zach jumped on the stage and started flexing his biceps like Hercules. The crowd loved it. They howled. I started thinking—"

"Count me in."

"Figured you were game...but this time we'll do it on Saturday night." Jonathan paused, then broke the silence with a snicker. "Buck, you'll get a charge out of this. There was a man at the show this afternoon who didn't appreciate Zach's performance. He was so steamed he came up the aisle cussing Zach and yelling, 'Get that guy off the stage. He's ruining the movie!' The more he complained, the more I laughed, and do you know who it was?"

Buck shook his head.

"It was the fellow who owns that car lot on Hunter Road. Talk about absurd—an old guy in a tie and suit, all alone at three in the afternoon, soaking up a Hercules flick. Didn't he have anything better to do? And what did he think was being ruined...a Hitchcock thriller? Zach's two minutes were better than the whole two hours of that low budget piece of junk he paid four bits to see."

"Well, look at it in a positive light. It's better for that guy to be down at the movies griping, instead of at his car lot fleecing a customer."

"Yeah, you've got a good point. I hear he's running a special on used Edsels. Anyhow, Buck here's the plan. Saturday night's performance will be Ed Sullivan quality, 'A really big *shew,*'" Jonathan said, talking like the 1950's television host. "Now, get a tee shirt, cut off the sleeves, and practice your routine in front of the mirror."

Buck lifted up his sleeve, flexing his muscle for a preview, revealing a slight bump on his toothpick thin arm. "Look at this."

"You're a born showman. And if you don't mind my saying so…you're gonna give'em a real bang for the *buck.*"

Buck frowned.

Friday, was a heavy duty recruiting day by the two promoters. "Spread the word! Saturday night. Holiday Theater. Randle will be on stage doing his Hercules bit!"

The reaction was varied. "You've got to be kidding." "I have to see this." Most shook their heads in unbelief. Still the consensus was "I'll be there."

Now there was nothing to do but wait—and hope that a heavy wind didn't blow Buck into the neighboring county. And he hoped that Joe didn't forget the cowbell—an imaginative last-minute addition to the extravaganza suggested by a friend.

Saturday night finally arrived. Jonathan was on duty and the movie started. As classmates continued filing into the theater and handing him their tickets, he heard comments like, "Is it still on?" "Is Randle gonna do it?"

Fortunately, his boss was nowhere within earshot. In truth, he rarely ever showed. It would be a terrible stroke of bad luck if he appeared. Jonathan factored that in. The odds were against it.

Five minutes before the big moment, Jonathan opened the door to the theater auditorium and surveyed a packed house. The only vacancies were a few seats near the front where Buck sat all alone, on the front row, left aisle.

Jonathan made his way toward his co-conspirator. As he walked, he heard a stirring among his classmates, most of whom occupied seats on the left side. He reached Buck and gave him his cue, noting the scene was only a few minutes away. Then he gave him a final encouragement, "This is the biggest crowd ever…and they're here to see you." He slapped him on the back. "Break a leg, Buck!"

As he headed back up the aisle, someone shouted, "Jonathan, when's it going to happen?" He held up three fingers, signaling the minutes until the big event. He continued toward the back. *This is great… Cecil B. DeMille must feel like this when he yells 'Lights! Camera! Action!'*

Then he saw her. Jenny sat near the one who shouted his name. She had a big smile on her face. As usual, a date was next to her, but it didn't matter because she was not smiling at her date—she smiled at

Jonathan, and it reinforced his excitement. This was his big moment, and Jenny was there.

Buck was the actor, but Jonathan was the producer and director. Suddenly, his high was threatened. *Jenny's watching. What if Buck flops?* His emotions plunged as the memory returned—the poem. *I was going to impress her then too.*

He closed his eyes, pleading within himself. *Come on Buck. Don't blow it.*

Buck did not flop. He was better than good—he was spectacular. He did more than a simple flexing of his biceps. He put his total anatomy into the performance. Before leaping onto the stage, Buck stripped off his jeans, revealing a swimsuit. His meager apparel enhanced the exhibition, stressing multiple parts of his less than eye-popping physique. The result was vintage, quintessential Buck. He was a combination of Olivier and Brando, with a little bit of Jerry Lewis thrown in. He milked the moment for all it was worth, and the crowd response was intoxicating.

Jonathan mentally played the scene over a dozen times before he finally went to sleep that night. Of course, the best thing of all, Jenny was there to see it. And he had caught her watching him, as she walked out of the theater.

Monday morning at school provided an even better moment. In between classes he saw Jenny coming down the hall. Although she was with someone else, as she normally was, she looked right at him even from a distance. She left her companion, and approached him.

"I couldn't believe what you did Saturday evening," she said. "It was hilarious. I laughed so hard, even after it was over I couldn't concentrate on the rest of the movie."

"You didn't miss anything," he assured her. "It wasn't *Casablanca*."

She laughed. "Bob was the one who told me you hatched the idea. I didn't know you did stuff like that. Bob says you were behind the Charlie Pitts thing too. "

"I'm guilty, but I wasn't alone. Buck was in on that one too…"

ಬಳಬಳ

John got up to walk down the aisle of the plane and stretch his legs. The cabin was nearly filled to capacity. Passengers talked, read, or watched the screen, except for a few who napped before dinner, like Max. As he returned to his seat, John continued his reverie, recalling how they dubbed it 'The Charlie Pitts Caper' and how Jenny had reacted to it…

The hoax was conceived one evening when he and Buck studied for Mr. Copeland's civics test. They hit it hard, digging into the textbook and looking through their scribbled notes scattered on Buck's dining room table. After a while, Jonathan became restless and couldn't concentrate.

"You know Buck, too much studying stunts the brain."

Buck nodded without looking up.

Jonathan put down his notes, walked over to the coffee table in the living room and picked up a book he noticed earlier. The title was an attention-getter, *Famous Outlaws of the Old West*. He sat down and skimmed it, flipping through the pages. This was much more interesting than what they were studying for civics—the rights and duties of citizenship. For some reason, reading about the crimes and capers against citizenry was far more entertaining. After examining the book for half an hour or so, Jonathan looked up and announced, "Buck, here's something about the famous Northfield, Minnesota bank robbery. Listen to this."

A disinterested Buck looked up. "This better be good."

"It is. You're gonna like this." Jonathan read a line.

"Fleeing the town under heavy gunfire, were the James brothers, Frank and Jessie, the Younger brothers, Cole, Jim and Bob, and Charlie Pitts."

"And here's another heist by the James gang," Jonathan continued. "While five of the outlaws fired pistols into the air, Jessie, Bob Younger, and Charlie Pitts, entered the bank."

Jonathan read several more accounts of crimes done by the gang, and each of them ended with the name Charlie Pitts. Buck finally broke into a laugh, because their thoughts ran in the same channel.

"I know what you're thinking, Jonathan…the James brothers I know, and the Youngers I've heard of, but who in Sam Hill is Charlie Pitts?"

"Actually, I was thinking, who in the Sam Hill is Sam Hill?" Jonathan said laughing. "But you're exactly right. What are we going to do with this Charlie Pitts character?"

Buck displayed a mischievous grin. "He does deserve his due recognition. Obviously, we're dealing with a gross miscarriage of justice."

"Actually, Buck, it's a travesty...historically speaking."

Bristling with feigned indignation, Buck continued to build their case. "He robs all these banks and trains, and what does he get...a mere footnote in history. We'll get Charlie Pitts his *rightful* place in the chronicles of men."

"Buck, them's my sentiments exactly. I think a simple grassroots strategy will work. Let's start dropping Charlie's name in casual conversation at school. We'll say stuff like, 'We were down at Walling's Creamery last night. Steve, Joe, and Kenneth were down there with Charlie Pitts.'"

"The guys will pick up on this real quick," Buck concurred. "The girls might take a little longer."

"Well, some of the girls will."

"Well, some guys too."

"You're right, Buck… you're always right."

"Say, Jonathan, couldn't this be considered a Civics class project? One of the duties of citizenship surely ought to be the pursuit of justice on behalf of a fellow citizen who has been wronged, namely Charlie Pitts. You think we could get extra credit for it?"

"Nope. Mr. Copeland isn't into these new progressive ideas in education."

Their plan quickly took off. Soon Charlie Pitts's name popped up everywhere. No one asked, "Who is Charlie Pitts?" Possibly, some thought he was like that invisible rabbit James Stewart ran around with in the *Harvey* movie. At any rate, Charlie's fame spread through school like a wildfire.

JENNY KISSED ME!

The local newspaper, *The San Marcos Record*, devoted a page each week to school events and activities. A column written by students covered the really important news items like "Who was that blond with Bruce at the drive-in Saturday night?"

Jonathan and Buck knew they made headway when, only two weeks into their crusade, the teen column carried the news that "Tollie and Bill were seen at Miller's Drive-in Saturday night in a car driven by Charlie Pitts." The conspirators roared with laughter because they had not planted this tidbit. The Pitts's campaign was in full swing, creating its own momentum.

The ultimate vindication of the forgotten highwayman occurred during the student council election. Buck and Jonathan walked down the hall, and in front of them a giant sign proclaimed:

Charlie Pitts will vote for Albert for Student Council President

Later he found out that Jenny, along with some of her friends, had made the poster. That was the best thing of all.

As they looked at the sign, both boys stood and delighted in their success. Nothing needed saying. They knew each other's thoughts. Mission accomplished. The truth was out. History had now liberated Charlie from the dustbins of obscurity.

"Buck," Jonathan confided, "we need to dump Chuck for his own good. We've got him involved in politics now, and that could soil his reputation. All our work could be for naught."

"Yeah," Buck said, "We sure didn't resurrect him to hook him up to a bunch of politicians. I'm sure he'd rather be remembered as a simple thief…"

∽∽∽

John chuckled aloud on the plane, just as he had done when Buck spoke those words in the hallway at high school. It had been great fun. But most of all Jenny had finally taken notice. He shook his head and glanced around to see if anybody noticed his laugh. Max was still asleep in the seat next to him, but it would soon be time for dinner and more conversation. One more image flitted through his memory, that of Jenny's face when she asked him about the Charlie Pitts Caper…

She stood there slowly shaking her head. Her facial expression was one that Jonathan had not seen before. Then she touched his hand and said. "Jonathan, there's more to you than I ever imagined." Before he could say a thing, she turned and danced away. At least it had seemed that way to him.

SIX

Long Summers

John finished his meal and turned to chat with his seatmate, Max. This time the subject was not literature. The topic turned to sports. John embraced the subject with only slightly less enthusiasm than poetry. Sports illustrations and metaphors were common in his classroom.

"Say, Max, since you're from Atlanta, have you ever made the trek to Augusta for the Masters?"

"I'm a regular. Wouldn't miss it for anything."

"You're a lucky guy. I know it's a tough ticket. It's a goal of mine someday to be close enough to see my reflection in Rae's Creek."

"Well, it's the highlight of *my* sports year."

"I'll go you one better," John responded. "I'm fanatical about basketball and football, mainly the college game, but I still believe the Masters is the single greatest sports event of the year."

"I agree, especially the final nine holes on Sunday. That's competitive drama at its best."

The conversation continued for a least thirty minutes as most sports, both amateur and professional, received at least passing attention. There was only one major disagreement. John argued that Tiger Woods would one day be recognized as the greatest golfer of all times. Max, however, contended that when all was said and done it would still be Jack Nicklaus.

"Max, were you there in '97 when Tiger set the record for the lowest 72-hole score? He won the tournament by twelve strokes—the youngest winner in history."

"You bet. And I was there in '86 when Nicklaus won the green jacket with a thirty on the back nine on the final day. He was the oldest winner in history and everybody thought he was washed up at age forty-six. Endurance, that's the mark of a champion. Tiger's a pup."

"Winning an argument with you, Max, is tougher than hitting a two iron," John said with a grin.

Max laughed. "You haven't met my wife." He yawned. "Well, it's about dark outside. The next time I see your mug, we'll be landing in Rome." Within seconds, he nodded off.

That was the cue John waited for. He closed his eyes and the memory journey picked up where he had left it—the day Jenny touched his hand and gave him that look…

JENNY KISSED ME!

He was so affected by it that he almost called her that evening for a date. He even dialed the first four digits of her telephone number, memorized months before. But his courage vanished. The impulse returned several times during their senior year, only to be repelled each time by the memory of the excruciating rejection he had experienced after revealing his heart their freshman year. He couldn't go through that again.

After the poem, his love for her had grown, not lessened. A second brushoff would have been unbearable. He couldn't chance it, knowing the odds of Jenny saying yes were so slim. *Why would the most gorgeous girl on the whole planet want a date with me?* And so he contented himself with just being friends. Visions of walking Jenny to the door for a goodnight kiss remained a pipe dream. Jonathan had to settle for the fantasy flights symptomatic of unrequited love. He understood the fanciful element in them, and he knew that his idyllic vision of Jenny had a mixture of the imaginary along with the real. She could not be perfect, but she was close...

Years later, John arrived at a more mature understanding of the nature of his experience. As a teacher of literature and poetry, he would inform his students, "Unrequited love presents none of the challenges, and reveals none of the flaws found in an actual relationship. You can idealize the Beloved, imagining her or him to be whatever you desire. After all, who can top a dream?"

ও৵ও৵ও৵

During the summer of 1959, Jonathan decided to cancel the fantasy flights for a season. They were becoming more pain than gain due to her prolonged absence from the scene. When each school year ended, Jenny sightings became rare—less than a dozen during the three summers following that first time he saw her. Most of the occasions were at the movies, or Rio Vista, a popular swimming spot on the river, or Walling's Creamery, the local malt shop. The moments were far too infrequent to suit his need. Looking at her picture helped, but it wasn't the same as seeing the living, breathing Jenny as she walked the halls, or sat in the classroom. By mid-July, he'd be noting the number of weeks before school reconvened. By the first week in August, he'd be counting the days, and by month's end, it would be the hours.

As his junior year drew to a close, he dreaded the thought of another summer. Each had seemed longer than the preceding. As he waved goodbye to Jenny on the last day of school, he resolved to fill the summer months with activity so there would be little time to think about her. First, he needed a job. That was nothing new, because he worked most summers, provided he found employment. This summer the need was supplied and came almost gift-wrapped only a couple of days after school ended.

"Jonathan, you want a job this summer?" The voice on the phone was Carroll, a classmate.

"You bet I do. I'm looking for something in an air-conditioned office with a desk and a secretary that looks like Elizabeth Taylor. Got anything?"

"Well, you can scratch the desk and office, and I think Liz is busy this summer. But we can do something about a cool work environment."

"I don't want to work at the ice house…too physical."

"Forget that. I'm talking about Wonder Cave. It's seventy-two degrees constant. What about being a tour guide? Summer is the busy season, so they need additional help. I trained for the job by going on tours the last three weekends. Now I'm taking my own, and they asked me if I could recommend anyone else who might be interested."

"Tell your boss I'm on my way."

Jonathan secured the job and started guiding tours two weeks later.

The following week, on a Sunday afternoon in early June, the second phase of the plan for a no-Jenny-summer materialized as he lay on a beach blanket, basking in the sun's rays at City Park. His friend Joe was next to him with a transistor radio in between. They were listening to one of those tear-jerker love songs, "It's Only Make Believe," sung by Conway Twitty. The words played on Jonathan's emotions as he identified with the singer, whose lyrics expressed the gut-wrenching experience of loving a girl who failed to return his affections.

Jonathan's thoughts turned to Jenny, and he realized his new job didn't completely solve his problem. It kept him busy during most daylight hours, but when the sun went down, visions of Jenny appeared with the night. The solution was soon to come as the radio played on.

> Summertime, baby, is the right time
> for people to fall in love.
> Every time I turn around, somebody's
> falling for love.

The song first caught his attention because a local rock band, The Traits, had recorded it. Two of the band members were in his class. His thoughts turned to the lyrics. The summer romance theme was a common one for that season of the year, but this time the message seemed to be directed right at him—a personal call to action. The lyrics set in motion a chain of events leading to the most incredible summer of his school years, culminating in the discovery of a poem about Jenny.

Immediately he sought solitude. "Joe, I'm going for a dip. Be back later...enjoy the rays."

Jonathan grabbed his inner tube and ran down the slope to the river. Minutes later, as he drifted in the current, his plan took shape. It had one limitation—he could not involve himself with a local high school girl since the relationship must terminate before the first school bell in the fall. Fortunately, San Marcos provided ample access to new girls. Every summer out-of-town chicks and their parents vacationed in cabins on the river. There was also the college. The girls who attended Southwest Texas State were older, but Jonathan didn't see it as a deterrent. He had seen many of them before at Walling's, and a number of them had looked his way. He figured age would be no problem.

JENNY KISSED ME!

Three days later, quite coincidentally, the plan was jump started on his day off. He and two friends, Rick and Randy, spent much of the afternoon sunning and swimming at Rio Vista before they dropped by Miller's Drive-In for a tall mug of frosted root beer. They were in Rick's car, and Jonathan occupied the passenger's seat.

Within moments, all three took notice of a brand new dark blue Chevy Impala, parked about thirty feet to the right. Business was slow, and no car blocked their view. They quickly realized the three occupants were not average looking girls.

Rick sized up the situation. "That's college stuff. Believe me, if they'd been walking the hallowed halls of San Marcos High we would have noticed."

"I'd say they range from about a seven point five to a nine," Jonathan chimed in.

"Yeah, you have to save the ten spot for Natalie Wood," Randy said.

"Or Kim Novak," Rick added.

Jonathan turned to Rick, "You got some paper?"

"Yeah, check the glove compartment."

"Rick, tap your horn. Get the carhop."

As the waitress turned toward the car, Jonathan motioned to her and she walked up to his window.

"Can I borrow your pencil?"

She raised one eyebrow.

"If you'll loan it to me, this guy behind me will give you a quarter. He thinks one of those girls in that blue Impala over there is a cousin he hasn't seen in a long time. He wants you to take this note I'm about to write, over to her."

"Yeah, sure," she said. "I don't buy that, but I'll do it anyway for gratis. I'm curious to see how this turns out."

Jonathan quickly scribbled a note, folded it, and handed it to the carhop. "Thanks. You'll get your quarter anyhow, plus…a fifty-cent commission if it works out."

As soon as she walked off, Randy asked, "What did you write? And by the way, I don't have a quarter."

"That's okay. I wrote we were very low on gas, probably driving on fumes…and would they mind taking up a collection to get us a dollars' worth of regular."

Randy buried his head in his hands. "You're kidding, right?"

"No, I'm not. Girls who look like that have heard every line in the book. You've got to be creative."

"You've been creative alright. You created an impossibility that we're ever goin' to get anywhere with those babes," Rick opined.

"Before you judge me, fellows, let this thing play out. Those gals may get a kick out of this. You've heard the expression, 'laughter is the way to a girl's heart.'"

"I've never heard that. Have you, Rick?"

"No."

"Well, neither have I," Jonathan confessed, "but I suspect somebody somewhere said it."

"Look!" Randy interrupted and pointed toward the Impala, "They're laughing."

The carhop, also laughing, turned and walked back toward them.

Jonathan said. "See, I told you guys. You should've trusted me."

"But are they laughing with us—or at us?"

"You've got a point, Rick." Then giving his friend a slight push on the shoulder, he added, "but I wish you had kept it to yourself."

The waitress arrived at Jonathan's window still laughing.

"Hold out your hand," she told Jonathan. "Here's ninety-three cents. They claimed it was all the money they had. By the way, the driver said tell you good luck."

"Wait, before you leave, could I borrow your pencil again?"

"Again?" She looked at him in astonishment.

"If you'll carry one more note over to them, the ninety-three cents is yours."

"Okay."

As the carhop left with the note, Rick asked, "What did you write this time, Kaelin?"

"I said the ninety-three cents was greatly appreciated, but if they felt bad about shorting us the seven cents, they could make it up by entertaining us in their beautiful blue car."

Randy was hesitant. "What if they find out we're only in high school, Jonathan?"

"We'll tell them we're about their same age because we were held back a couple of grades."

"That'll sure impress them," Rick said cynically.

Then they saw the driver motion for them to come over.

"Let's go guys," Jonathan encouraged, "we'll play this by ear. Fortune favors the bold."

He led the way, walking up to the driver's window and peering into the front seat. "Bench seats...perfect for six. Don't you girls get the feeling this was meant to be?"

Just that quick they were all in the Impala, laughing and having a ball. Right away, the girls discovered they were high school boys, but it didn't seem to matter.

Jonathan was instantly attracted to the driver, and he overturned the lowest ranking he had earlier assigned her. The appeal was not her car, though he could picture himself at the wheel. It was her personality—deserving of a ten. He had never met a girl with a sense of humor so similar to his own. Her name was Karen. She had just entered college that summer, following her graduation from a south Texas high school three weeks earlier.

After about an hour together, the girls had to return to campus for their evening meal.

As Jonathan got out of Karen's Chevy, he calculated the situation. *"It's Now or Never," as Elvis would say.*

He walked around to the driver's side. "Karen, could you write down your phone number for me, in case we run low on gas again." He grinned. "You damsels are good at rescuing guys in distress."

Karen complied, handing it to Jonathan with a big smile.

Three hours later the two of them were on the phone, and Jonathan asked for a date.

JENNY KISSED ME!

"Here's the way I figure it, Karen. You tell your friends you're robbing the cradle. I'll tell my friends I'm dating an older woman. It'll be a scandal. Let's do it."

"Do I pick you up, or do you have a car?" she asked.

"I'll have one tomorrow night, but I might take you up on the offer some other time."

So the summer romance was underway. Karen provided the transportation most of the time, and whenever Jonathan drove the Impala he was on the lookout for friends he could greet with a showy wave. Most of all he hoped to see Jenny, but he never did. Buddies called him that summer to ask about the car and the girl. His answer never varied—delivered with the same nonchalance, "It's her car...I'm dating an older woman." When he hung up the phone, he'd always laugh.

His plan worked and the summer flew by.

Then something happened during Karen's final evening in San Marcos, something which caused Jonathan to realize the plan had not been flawless.

He and Karen were eating banana splits at Walling's when Jonathan turned his head and saw Jenny and Sandra—heading straight for their table.

Jenny spoke first. "Haven't seen you all summer, Jonathan. What have you been up to?"

"Raising chicken hawks."

"What? Why?"

Jonathan shrugged his shoulders and looked confused. "Beats the heck out of me."

Jenny detected that mischievous gleam in his eye, and they both broke into laughter.

"He's crazy," Karen said as she looked over at Jenny.

"I know," Jenny said, glancing back at Jonathan. For a brief moment, their eyes locked in a shared realization that the summer had been too long.

Sandra broke the silence. "Jenny, let's go to the back room and see if anybody's dancing."

Jenny's eyes lingered a few seconds longer. She touched his shoulder as she passed by. "Jonathan, I'll see you in two weeks."

Karen and Jonathan hardly spoke on their way back to the campus. As they parked across from her dormitory, she asked, "Are you going to come down and see me before school starts? I want you to meet my family."

Jonathan said nothing.

Karen continued, "I didn't tell you, but I've had a boyfriend back home. We went steady our last two years in high school. He decided not to go to college. He's learning his father's business, you know, so he can take it over later. I called him and told him about you."

Jonathan had a sick feeling in the pit of his stomach. He had nothing clever to say. He knew he was about to hurt someone he cared a great deal about, someone who had become very special that summer. The words didn't come.

Karen broke the silence. "It's the girl at Walling's isn't it. What's her name? Jenny?"

Jonathan looked out the window. "You've found me out, Karen. I'm sorry. How could you tell?"

"You lit up when she walked over to the table."

"I did?"

"Yes…you looked at her in a way you've never looked at me." Karen laid her hand on his shoulder. "I wish you had."

For the first time since they left the ice cream shop, Jonathan looked at Karen. The words formed slowly and painfully. "It's been like that…since the first time I saw her…in the ninth grade."

Looking out into the night Karen asked, "Does she know it?"

"No, you're the only one who does. Once I tried to tell her, but it didn't work."

There was momentary silence. "She likes you, I can tell."

"As a friend, yeah, but that's all."

The dormitory lights blinked.

"I've got to go, Jonathan."

When they reached the top of the steps, Karen quickly headed for the door.

"Karen, please…," Jonathan pleaded.

She stopped and looked back with tears in her eyes. He reached out, put his arms around her; and spoke softly, "Since I first saw Jenny, there was never a day I didn't think of her—until these last few months…when I was with you. This has been the most unforgettable summer of my life." Then he kissed her, turned and walked slowly down the steps, emotions plunging with each descent. As he drove away, his condition did not improve. By the time he braked for the red light on the square, the pain was acute. He realized he would have exchanged all the fun and laughter of the past two and a half months for another lonely summer without Jenny, if it would have taken away the hurt he saw in Karen's eyes. Hurt that he had inflicted.

He tried to assuage his guilt by convincing himself that had he known of her boyfriend back home he never would have allowed it to go this far. But still he was bothered by a pang of conscience over having deceived Karen, leading her to believe that their relationship was something more permanent. For him, it had been a summer's game. A lark. He hadn't considered the effect it would have on her. For a moment, he tested other waters in an attempt to ease the anguish. He even started to blame Jenny. *If it wasn't for her I never would've done this in the first place.* His rationalization was short-lived. He knew better. *Jenny is beautiful and sweet. She can't help that, but I should be able to control how I feel about her.*

Jonathan was about to pull into his garage, but something stopped him. Impulsively he backed out of the driveway and headed across town—to a familiar place. On the way, a painful reality struck as he became aware that he had not conveniently dropped out of the game unscathed. He too would bear wounds. The whisperings on the dorm steps spoke loudly the feelings of his heart. He would not forget these last few months. A casual summer romance had unexpectedly become his first matter of the heart. Jenny was only make-believe. Karen was real. She had loved back.

He pulled his car into Sewell Park. The summer had issued so many remembrances of Karen: movies at the downtown theater, Friday nights at the drive-in, and downing malts and splits at Walling's Creamery while they listened to the jukebox. But the best moments of the memorable summer together were those off days and early afternoons before work spent at the park, sunbathing and swimming, tubing, playing table tennis, and walking hand in hand by the river bank.

He looked over at a spot near the water, and he thought of the evening they had taken their beach towels and spread them on the ground. The stars were out full. They had kissed a few times, but mostly marveled at God's handiwork above, holding hands, talking and laughing, enjoying one another's company. Now as he looked at the very spot they had shared together, a terrible sadness swept over him. A wonderful time in his life had ended.

When he returned home, a despondent Jonathan entered his room and instinctively headed for the bookshelf. He had discovered early on, reading poetry, like listening to good music was a means of deliverance from the doldrums. This time he knew top-of-the-line help was desperately needed. His eyes focused on the shelf where his favorite book, *The Best-Loved Poems of the American People,* stood. His love affair with poetry had begun within its pages half a dozen years earlier. He took it from the shelf and gripped it tight with both hands. Pausing, he reflected on some of the beauty and insights he had found within its covers. The book was a sizable volume, over six hundred pages, so he had not read all of its offerings. He usually ignored the topical sections of minimal interest to him. Otherwise, his approach had been without scheme, allowing his eyes to fall on whatever poem came into view as he spread the book open.

He waited with anticipation. He had experienced it so many times—that expectancy that he was about to discover something wonderful within its pages. The book fell open at page six. And there it was. He looked away, and then looked down again in amazement. It was not an illusion. It was real. Those three words near the bottom of the page were all capitalized—JENNY KISSED ME.

SEVEN

The Kiss

Jonathan hesitated, determined to savor the moment. *This can't be happening. It's too perfect.* And then a quick reversal—*What if this is from the* Humor and Whimsy *section? I sure don't want a funny poem about Jenny. She's no laughing matter.* He forced himself to look at the top of the page and his anxiety eased when he saw the subtitle, *Love and Friendship*. He was in the right place. Since it was his favorite section, he wondered how he could have missed it.

Initially he imagined two pages must have stuck together, but upon examination he eliminated that possibility. Then he glanced at the poem situated above and solved the mystery. Printed at the top of the page was "She Walks in Beauty"—one of the most famous romantic poems ever written.

He looked at the opening words of Byron's masterpiece. Since he had memorized that poem in the seventh grade, after first reading it, there had been no need to return to it. Even if he had, the name Jenny below it would have meant nothing to him then.

Once again he looked at the title and paused. *This…was written for me.*

> Jenny kissed me when we met,
> Jumping from the chair she sat in.

Jonathan stopped reading and stared at the words in utter amazement. He just knew the poem would live up to the promise its lofty title merited. Then very slowly, he continued. He wanted somehow to stretch a very short poem of eight verses into an epic. Finally, it ended with the perfect crescendo.

> Say I'm weary, say I'm sad;
> Say that health and wealth have missed me;
> Say I'm growing old, but add—
>   Jenny kissed me!

Jonathan committed the poem to memory in less than five minutes. He drank in every syllable of every word as he visualized the scene. Never had he put such total focus and passion into memorization. This was an anthem to Jenny. For days after, it played over and over in his mind. Then eight months later the words came to life.

JENNY KISSED ME!

The supreme Jenny moment happened in the library about two months before the conclusion of his senior year. Jonathan had an off period before lunch, as was true of a number of his friends. He was on his way to the gym, eager to find some guys to shoot baskets when he ran into Graham.

"Jonathan, I just heard your name."

"Hope it wasn't the principal."

"Nope, it was Jenny. I saw her in the library. She mentioned you."

"Was she by herself?"

"No, there were a bunch of girls with her."

"Really." Jonathan's voice fell.

"You know the crowd… Diane, Lynn, Laura. Joann was there too. They were studying for an English test, and Jenny said, 'I wish Jonathan was here. He's into literature and poetry, and he could help us.'"

"What did you say?"

Graham shrugged. "I said, you mean the poetry reading contest? He did that for kicks. They made him do it. He doesn't know any more about that mush than I know about open-heart surgery. But Jenny said, 'You just don't know.'" Graham looked puzzled. "What was she talking about?"

"I'm not sure," Jonathan said as he walked away.

"Where're you headed?"

"I'm going to mosey over to the library. I may not be able to help, but the surroundings sound great. Plenty of pretty girls."

As he headed to the library, Jonathan was somewhat bothered by his pretended ignorance. By the

113

time he arrived, he had rationalized, *Graham just wouldn't understand.*

Jonathan spotted Jenny and the other girls at a table with their heads buried either in a book or their notes. He decided to play it coy. He would not approach Jenny yet. Parking himself at the history section within her eyesight, he randomly pulled a book off the nearest shelf, sat down, and opened it. When he noticed the content, he longed for a quick deliverance. The hastily grabbed book was about the prehistory period, entitled *Stone Age Man.* He looked at the chapter headings—Paleolithic Age, Mesolithic Age. He liked history, but he loathed this stuff. It was about mankind before the invention of writing. Jonathan had a simple theory about those preliterate times. *If humans living then had something interesting to say, they would have invented a way to say it.* He casually flipped the pages, reading a paragraph here and there. He thought Jenny would never notice him and come over.

After what seemed forever, he looked over the top of the book and their eyes met. Jenny stood and walked over to his table and sat next to him.

"Jonathan, are you studying for the English Lit test?"

"No, I'm just reading."

"What's the book about?"

"*The Theory of Relativity*, by Al Einstein."

"Really? Do you understand that stuff?"

"What do you think." He grinned. "Do I look like the sort? That kind of thing fills the air across the hall while we're pounding typewriter keys." He pushed the book aside and said, "I'm just killing time. Off period, you know."

"Jonathan, I'm really worried about our test, especially the poetry part. I've only made one 'B' in high school. All the rest have been 'A's. I'm hoping for a scholarship…I can't bear another 'B'."

"I could sure bear it. My problem is trying to make a 'B'."

Jenny smiled. "I know better than that. And you've had lots more fun than I have, with all your shenanigans—Hercules, and Charlie Pitts, and all that. What else have you pulled?"

"That's highly classified information. It won't be released until I'm out of here, diploma in hand."

Aware of her anxiety about the exam, he changed the subject, "Can I help you?"

"Do you think Mr. Williams will give us an essay test?"

"Count on it. That's all he can do, dealing with this kind of material."

"What if he asks when the Romantic period began? When I look at my notes, they're really confusing."

"That means you took good notes, Jenny."

She laughed. "What do you mean?"

"It's confusing because even literary historians disagree about that. They don't even agree on exactly how to define it."

"Then how would you answer it?"

"I think I'd go to the next question."

"Please, Jonathan, stop teasing. I need help."

"Okay. Let's start with the definition. The Romantic writers usually emphasize stuff like imagination, intuition, and feeling. It applies to art and music of the period as well as the poetry."

"Music…like Beethoven?"

"Uh-huh, an early nineteenth century piece by Beethoven is frequently recognized as the beginning of Romantic music."

"What about poetry—Keats, and Shelley?"

"They're Romantics, all right, but they come later, kind of a second wave. Some historians will go back as far as the 1780s for the beginning of the movement, with guys like Burns. That's Robert, not George."

Jenny giggled. "I'm glad you made that clear."

"There is a significant date to remember about the period. It's 1798. That's when Wordsworth and Coleridge published *Lyrical Ballads*."

"Didn't Coleridge write the *Rime of the Ancient Mariner*?"

"Right. And it's in that very book."

"Amazing. How'd you learn all this?"

Jonathan faked a sigh, "During my elementary years, I often stayed after school for cutting up in class. I was forced to read poetry books as punishment. Here my friends were, outside playing ball, while I was inside, learning how to pronounce iambic pentameter."

Jenny laughed and then said, "I never know when you're joking or serious, Jonathan. What if all this jazz you've been talking about is something you made up."

Jonathan's demeanor changed. "Jenny," he paused, "I think you know when I'm serious."

The words were unplanned, followed by a dead silence between them. Jonathan knew what past occasion had prompted the words, and by the look in her eyes, she knew too.

"Anyway," Jonathan advised, "mention *Lyrical Ballads* on your test, as the beginning of the period. Some scholars believe that. Even if Mr. Williams doesn't buy it, the information will impress him. In an essay test, if you give the teacher some specifics, even if it's not exactly what he's looking for, you'll get some credit. But if he detects you're trying to cover up your ignorance with a rambling snow job, then that 'A' will go the way of *homo erectus pekinensis*."

Jenny shook her head, "What in the world are you talking about?"

"Peking Man…it's right here in this book." He tapped the cover of *Stone Age Man* with his forefinger. "This isn't really by Einstein. The author mentions the fossil remains of a man found in China in the 1920's. He's older than Einstein."

"Jonathan, you're a nut. But a brilliant nut. Thanks for helping me, I knew you would."

"Don't worry, Jenny. You'll do great."

She got up and walked away. Suddenly she stopped, turned, and made her way back to Jonathan's table.

His eyes had followed her and questioned why she came back.

She looked at him with that same expression he had seen once before when she touched his hand. She did it again. Laying her hand on top of his, she said, "You know who my favorite poet is?"

"Ogden Nash?"

"No…you are!"

117

Then it happened. She leaned over and kissed him on the cheek. They looked at one another for a few seconds and said nothing. Afterward, as if coming out of a daze, she smiled and slowly walked away.

Jonathan remained at the table thunderstruck until the girls left. Unaware of the time, he stared mindlessly at the library book, barely able to contain his emotions, as he thought over, and over, ***Jenny kissed me!***

ം‍ം‍ം

Hours later, Jonathan lay on his bed, determined to stay awake and soak up every ounce of pleasure from the pinnacle Jenny moment. It was impossible to express the feelings that swirled within him. A poem flashed into his mind. He had memorized it at one of his silly moments. He smiled. Maybe it wasn't so silly after all.

> *I climbed up the door,*
> *and opened the stairs*
> *I said my pajamas,*
> *and put on my prayers*
> *I turned off the bed,*
> *and crawled into the light*
> *And all because you kissed me goodnight.*

Jonathan was careful not to wash his cheek that night. He knew he would need to eventually, but perhaps he would die first. If that happened, he wouldn't have very far to go. He was already halfway to heaven.

EIGHT

Leftover Dreams

A couple sitting down in the airplane seats next to Jenny interrupted her thoughts about Jonathan and summoned her back into the moment. They appeared older than she, probably in their mid-60s. The woman seated herself next to Jenny, whose perfume-counter senses perceived the elegance of *Chanel No. 5*. Before the plane was even in flight the three were already talking. Jenny rarely had difficulty initiating a conversation, and she quickly found out, neither did her new acquaintances, Kay and Bud Garner. Only minutes into the chitchat, all were surprised and delighted by discovering their good fortune of being in the same tour group.

The three talked for most of an hour. Much of it was spent laughing. Both Bud and Kay had a great sense of humor, which included playfully teasing each other. Their laugh fest came to an end when Bud announced, "Ladies, I've got to retire. A man my age needs his sleep. You two girls will look just as good without it."

Kay smiled and looked over at Jenny. "Isn't he sweet?"

Then, determined to conclude with a good-natured gibe, Bud added, "After all, look at all that junk you put on your face. It gives you an edge, don't you think."

"You just couldn't stop could you," Kay said, handing him his sleep mask. "I thought you were going to sleep." Before he could answer, she added, "We won't miss your conversation. We have girl talk to do. Might even put cosmetics on our agenda."

The two women talked about twenty minutes, mostly about trivia. Then noticing Bud was sound asleep, Jenny got more personal. "Kay, I can tell you two are crazy about each other." Gesturing toward Bud she added, "He's quite a character."

The tone of Kay's voice took on a serious quality. "He is a character, Elaine, but more importantly," she spoke the words with emphasis and clarity, "he *has* character. He was a building contractor for years, just retired last April. He had a plaque in his office that said, 'Fame is a vapor, Popularity an accident, Riches take wings. Only one thing endures, and that is character.'" She glanced lovingly at her husband. "Those words have a lofty ring, but Bud actually lives them. He always has."

"You're fortunate that you found a man like that, Kay. How'd you meet?"

"We grew up together."

"Childhood sweethearts?"

"No, just childhood friends. We became sweethearts later. That took time."

"I'd love to hear about it."

"Well, Bud and I grew up on the same street, a few houses apart. I can't remember when I didn't know him. He was two years older than me, the same age as my brother Gary. The two of them were inseparable, so Bud was like a member of our family."

"What changed it?"

"One summer when I was in the fifth grade, Gary was at our grandparents' farm for a couple of weeks, so I was playing alone in front of our house. Two older boys, who didn't live in our neighborhood, spotted me while they walked by and started bothering me. They grabbed my bicycle. I think they intended to steal it, so I screamed. Bud heard it and came running to my rescue."

"Wow."

"I can still see Bud lighting into both of them. They blooded him up, but he never quit."

"Did they get your bicycle?"

"No! I think they would've had to kill Bud to get it. And they must've known it," Kay laughed. "They finally left... they were bloody too."

"He was your knight errant. How romantic!"

Kay nodded and smiled.

"Did that make him your sweetheart?"

"Not yet, but he sure was my hero."

"Well, what did it take?" Jenny urged.

"Later, he went to school in a nearby city, while I attended the local college. I dated a number of guys in high school and college. I even had several steady boyfriends, so I knew what was out there. One day I was at a girlfriend's apartment along with some other friends. Bud and some of his college cronies walked in. He'd brought them home for the weekend and one of them knew my girlfriend. Anyway there was quite a group there. We spent the evening talking, laughing, swapping stories. You might guess who the big hit of the evening was—kept everybody in stitches."

"Bud."

"I was sitting on the floor looking up at him as he stood there telling one of his funny stories. Like a bolt from the blue, it struck me that I loved him. I hardly said a word the rest of the evening." She giggled. "You've probably figured out that's not easy for me."

"I can identify with that."

"Anyway, after the guys left, one of my friends started raving about Bud and asked me to arrange a date for her. I said, 'No...he's mine!' My friend said, 'I didn't know that.' And I said, 'Neither does *he*—not yet.'"

Jenny laughed. "I've got to hear the rest of this. How did you let him know?"

"I asked my brother to set me up on a blind date. Gary had a steady girlfriend at the time, named Peggy. She was also a good friend of mine, so he could honestly say to Bud 'Peggy has a friend I want you to go out with.'"

"How did Bud react when he saw you?"

"He took it all as a joke and laughed. We had a great time. I didn't let on until he took me home and we sat on the porch swing."

"What did you say?"

"I put my hand on his cheek and said, 'Bud, I have a confession to make. I arranged all this. You know why?' He joked, 'You wanted to see that movie, and all of your boyfriends were broke?' 'No,' I told him, 'I love you and I want to marry you!' I still can see his expression. For the first and only time, he was utterly speechless."

"What then?" Jenny asked excitedly.

"You need to realize, I'd rehearsed this a half dozen times in my mind. I was determined to say the right thing. There was too much at stake." Kay looked over adoringly at her husband, who now snored softly. "Anyway, I told him, 'You can run after other girls, but you'll never find anyone who will love you as much as I do. I've put more into it. I've loved you since I was ten years old and you saved my bicycle.' I kissed him and headed for the front door. When I looked back, there he sat, staring straight ahead, totally baffled—and still speechless."

"Weren't you concerned about him not saying anything, Kay?"

"No I wasn't, I was sure no girl had ever shut him up before, so I figured that was a good sign."

"What happened then?"

"The next evening he called and asked me out. A year later, after his graduation, we were married."

Jenny reached over and squeezed Kay's hand. "Thanks for a lovely story. I just can't believe you were so bold. Girls weren't usually that forward back then. I admire you for it."

Kay looked over at Bud again. "I wasn't going to let him get away." She lightly rested her hand on his arm. "Not any more than he was going to let those boys take my bicycle."

"I envy both of you, Kay, you have something special."

"I hope you haven't thought I'm crazy, sharing all of this with a stranger, but Elaine, it feels like we're old friends already."

Jenny smiled and said, "I feel like that too."

"Well at least, let me tell you why I've carried on so. Today's a special day. It's our fortieth wedding anniversary."

Jenny's eyes lit up. "Really?" She turned toward Kay. "I'm so happy for you."

"But that's not all of it. On our twentieth, I began a tradition—just for me. I decided I would spend some part of the anniversary day each year doing nothing but remembering…things like I shared with you." She nodded her head toward Bud. "It helps to remind me how grateful I am for him, and how right I was in going after him." She patted Jenny's hand. "You're the unfortunate one—putting up with my nostalgic ramblings."

"Those ramblings are my treat. Going to Italy for your fortieth is really something. Congratulations!"

"We did it on our twentieth and thirtieth, too."

"And you still enjoy it?"

"We enjoy it more every time. There's always something new, and we get a kick out of recalling experiences we've had on earlier trips." Kay giggled. "Elaine, if you tag along with us, you're certain to hear 'Do you remember the last time we were at this place.'"

"Is that an invitation?"

"Absolutely! We'd love to have you."

Kay removed her glasses, put them in her purse, and said, "I'd better catch up on the sleep I lost last night, from four decades of memories. I think it was about 3 a.m. before I drifted off." She leaned her head back, fixing her eyes on a void. In time, the words came out, barely audible, "What if I'd never told him my feelings." Then, she closed her eyes, and her voice trailed off. "What if …."

Jenny made no verbal response, because her mind started to drift, triggered by the story of Bud and the bicycle. His heroics brought to mind an occasion where she learned of a similar act of valor by Jonathan. It was at her second class reunion, two years after her divorce.

Jenny cherished those reunions, at least the earlier ones It was fun to talk about old times, and interesting to see the changes in her classmates—in looks and occasionally in personality.

The most extreme personality change had to be a boy named Oliver, or as they called him back then "Oliver the Obnoxious"—not to his face, of course. But it was an appropriate tag, for if they had voted someone the title of Most Offensive, he would have won in a landslide. Even Jenny, who tended to look for the best in everyone, had to admit that no matter how hard you looked for good in Oliver, there was none to find. There was only Oliver...

Now twenty years after graduation, the word was out that Oliver was a missionary. When Jenny became aware of this fact, her curiosity got the best of her and she decided to seek him out. Spotting him alone, she approached. They talked for fifteen minutes or so, and she decided that he really had changed. He seemed like a genuinely nice person—quite a metamorphosis.

She was about to move on to another classmate when Oliver asked, "Hey Jenny, you remember a boy named Jonathan, don't you?"

"Sure. Why?"

"Let me tell you a story about him. It involves you."

"Me?"

"You probably remember what a jerk I was in high school."

Jenny managed to let that moment pass in silence.

"I know I was a real clod. Anyway, one time I made a crude comment about you to Jonathan. You know how boys sometimes talk about girls. I'm sorry now for what I said, but at the time, *he* made me sorry in a different way. He decked me right there in the hallway, for everyone to see."

Jenny looked at Oliver, as if a puzzling mystery had suddenly been solved.

"I remember that!" she exclaimed. "I knew about Jonathan getting in a fight. It was our junior year. I was down the hall when it happened. We were all surprised. It was so unlike him."

"Well, now you know why. It was about you."

She shook her head. "I had no idea."

JENNY KISSED ME!

Taken aback by the revelation, but not knowing what to say, Jenny tried to end the conversation. "Oliver, I'm really happy for the way your life has turned out...and thanks for sharing the story."

"And Jenny, I bet there's another thing you never knew about Jonathan. The guy could really punch." He grinned and pointed to a small scar on his lip. "I bear permanent evidence."

Jenny smiled and turned to leave, but Oliver stopped her again, placing his hand lightly on her shoulder. "Do you know why I told you that story?"

"No."

"I needed to talk about Jonathan. He was the person I most wanted to see at this reunion. Since he's not here, I'll tell you."

Jenny looked at him curiously.

"After the fight, I had to admire him for the reason he did it. You see, he warned me not to tell anybody. He did it to defend your honor—that's all that mattered to him." Oliver looked at her intently. "There was something different about Jonathan, and it even affected me back then. I just wish he was here so I could tell him."

He paused and said, "Jenny do you know where he is?"

She shook her head, "No, Oliver, I haven't seen him since graduation day." As Jenny walked away, she heard the words, "I think he loved you..."

The next day after the reunion as Jenny left San Marcos to return home, she reflected on her meeting with Oliver, especially the words he had spoken as she left him. Thoughts of Jonathan returned. *I wonder if he's married? I wonder where he lives? Why didn't he come to the reunion?*

By the time she arrived at her Dallas home, one desire dominated her emotions. She had to see Jonathan's picture in her annual. She hadn't seen the book in years, and her diligent search proved fruitless. That day was the final time she thought of him until the eventful day she held his letter in her hands two decades later.

ഇഇഇ

Jenny yawned and realized she was finally getting sleepy. Before she adjusted her pillow, she took a final glance at her new friend, now sound asleep. She couldn't help being a little envious of the memories Kay had shared about the man she loved.

As sleepiness came, Jenny's thoughts began to fade amid a longing for such memories. She had none, only the leftover dreams of what might have been, spawned by Kay's final words, *"What if..."*

NINE

November 1963

Jenny had talked about attending the University of Texas the evening she danced with Jonathan at the prom. That was in the spring of 1960, and at the time she assumed the school's proximity to San Marcos meant she would return often to her hometown. However, after she arrived on the Austin campus, those expectations vanished. Given her effervescent personality and social nature, she quickly blended into campus life. One evening following a football game, six weeks into the first semester, she stood in the midst of an ever increasing bevy of friends. They were all gazing at the University of Texas Tower, now bathed in orange light following a victory, when she exclaimed loud enough for all to hear, "I love college. I could stay here forever."

Thoughts of home, even returning for a quick visit, vanished. She called her mom and dad once a week, and would see them when they came into Austin. However, weekends were full of activity with parties, movies, and sports events. Dates were easy to come by. Jenny never went anywhere alone. By the time the fall semester ended, she did not even return home for the holidays until Christmas Eve. Skiing in Colorado with new friends held greater attraction.

A month deep into that spring's semester, she settled on a steady. His name was Teller, a boy she would later marry. Thoughts of the hometown boy who had stolen her heart with a poem became a faded memory.

༺༻

It had not been the same for Jonathan. Physically, he was in San Marcos, but his heart was in Austin where Jenny lived—just thirty miles north on Interstate 35. During the empty weekends of his first college semester, Jonathan drove by Jenny's parents' house, hoping to see her car in the driveway. He never did. When Christmas break began, after he drove by her house for three consecutive days and saw no sign of her presence, he resolved to forget her once and for all. It was one thing to dream of her during high school, when at least he saw her. Now, it was different. Though still vivid in his thoughts, she was nowhere present. *Why pursue a phantom?*

Jonathan submerged his thoughts and energies into a multiplicity of activities—he pledged a fraternity, got involved in intramural sports, started dating—and of course there were academics. Dating was relatively new to Jonathan, except for that summer with Karen. He had occasionally dated in high school, but it was mainly for special school events. His heart belonged to Jenny. Now, determined to alter that, he proceeded on his new course with fervor. There were even weekends when he set up dates with more than one girl.

Shortly after he launched into the dating scene, Jonathan attempted to locate Karen by contacting her roommate from that summer. Candis was from the same hometown. She informed him that Karen quit school following her freshman year, went home, and married her high school sweetheart.

"It took her a few months to get over you, Jonathan—but she finally did."

"That's great. I'm happy for her. Please tell her. And tell her I think her husband's a lucky man." As Jonathan walked away, he was pleased at the news.

ഌഌഌ

Jonathan never regretted the myriad moments he spent absorbed with Jenny in high school. He came to look upon those years philosophically, thinking of a Bible verse he heard growing up: "When I was a child, I spake as a child, I understood as a child, I thought as a child: but when I became a man, I put away childish things."

Jenny was relegated to Jonathan's childhood. He was in college now. She belonged to the past. Jenny was a page which had been turned. His vow to forget her was honored, at least consciously, for the next three years. Then in November of 1963, as fate would have it, a phone call from an old high school buddy reintroduced Jenny into his life.

Following Buck's graduation from San Marcos High, he left for College Station and Texas A&M on a partial track scholarship as a long distance runner. Jonathan had been a University of Texas fan for as long as he could remember, and his allegiance to the school increased knowing Jenny was on campus. However, the bitter rivalry between UT and A&M did not inhibit his friendship with good ol' Buck. But Thanksgiving—the traditional day when the two schools met on the gridiron—was a horse of a different color. Burnt orange and maroon definitely clashed.

As Jonathan picked up the phone, he perked up at the sound of his friend's voice. After the customary chit chat, Buck prepared him for a surprising gift.

"Jonathan, is it true you've never seen a *T.U.* game in person?"

"Did you call just to rub that in? Tickets are hard to come by for this tapped out college boy. Remember Buck, I didn't get to go away to school like you rich guys."

"Well, if a tea-sip sympathizer like you isn't too proud to take a handout from this rich Aggie, we can fix this. I've scrounged up two tickets, absolutely free."

Jonathan burst out, "One for me?"

"No, you get both of them. I can't sit with you. I'm in the Corps. Why don't you get Tollie to go with you?"

"How'd you come up with them?"

"Well, it wasn't like I had to run a four minute mile. They're hardly scarce."

132

JENNY KISSED ME!

"Yeah, you Aggies aren't exactly having a banner year, are you? I'm sorry, you did win one game...didn't mean to slight you."

"Keep it up and these tickets will end up in the bonfire. I know your team is undefeated, but no flaunting. Let's hear a little humility."

"Alright I take it back, but tell me something."

"Let's hear it."

"What's an Aggie doing lecturing someone on humility?"

Buck snickered. "At any rate there are tickets available this year. Some of our people have decided to stay home and watch the slaughter on TV."

"Buck, you're a real buddy. Thank you. But," Jonathan paused and reminded him, "don't forget I made you legendary in the annals of San Marcos High."

"The 'Hercules' bit?"

"How soon you forget the favors of a friend."

"Enough. You've got the tickets. But, you know you'll be surrounded by Aggies. In Kyle Field, you're the enemy."

"I'll manage. I've put up with you for the last three year."

The first five minutes after he hung up the phone, Jonathan thought of nothing but the football game and its implications. He was not only going to see his beloved Longhorns play live and in person, but by game day he fully expected the University of Texas to be ranked number one in the polls. A national championship could be on the line. If that were the case, it would be their first in history, and he could not imagine the game at Kyle Field as anything but a Texas victory. Suffering a loss in the midst of Aggie taunts would be unthinkable, but it just couldn't happen to this Longhorn juggernaut against a team having such a pathetic year. This would to be an unforgettable experience.

Then a thought struck, and elation soared to sheer ecstasy.

Jenny is a Longhorn cheerleader!

He suspected that all of San Marcos knew. When a local girl becomes a cheerleader at the state's flagship university, it's big news. But had you asked anyone in her hometown if the selection was a surprise, the consensus response would have been in the negative.

༄༅༄

The teakettle whistled cheerily as Jonathan dashed from his room, dressed for his first class of the day. As usual, he purposefully slept as late as possible, and then managed to slip into his desk seconds before the professor entered the classroom. There was no time for breakfast—just a hastily prepared cup of instant coffee and a cursory look at the front page of the *Austin American-Statesman* laying on his mom's kitchen table. As Jonathan headed for the back door, he made an uncharacteristic stop to consult the calendar on the wall next to the door. It was Friday, November 22nd, 1963. Placing his finger on the 28th, he spoke in a low voice, lips partly closed, "Only six days to go…a Jenny moment."

It seemed like an eternity since he had seen her—graduation night… May 28, 1960… eighteen minutes after nine. When he walked away from her that evening, he never imagined it would be so long before he would see her again. Stepping into the garage, he spoke her name louder than before, "Jenny, I've missed you."

As he drove to class, thoughts of her were momentarily replaced by thoughts of the newspaper headlines he had scanned. President Kennedy was to arrive in Austin from Dallas just after three that afternoon on Air Force One. Darrell Royal, Texas' football coach, was selected to greet the first family and present the president with an autographed team football.

As impressed as Jonathan was with the Longhorn's head coach, he couldn't help thinking. *I would have picked the head cheerleader to present the football.*

Jonathan's excitement accelerated that morning as the hours passed. Taking class notes, periodically interrupted by flashbacks of Jenny, was a challenge. He knew his view of her would be limited—through the lenses of binoculars—but still, after all of this time the sight would be blissful. The anticipation forced him to admit that he had deluded himself into believing he had forgotten her. He had simply driven the memory of her deeper into his soul. He understood now why he played the field when he began dating midway through his freshman year at SWT. He never had more than three dates with any one girl. Whenever he detected seriousness, he eased up on the relationship. There was always the hope of Jenny.

The memory of her was never more alive than when the music stopped. He had gone home for lunch and started back to campus for afternoon classes, listening to a San Antonio rock and roll station on the car radio. They were playing a song which had been popular several years before. Most of the '50s songs brought memories with them—people, places, and occasions. Of course, memories of Jenny topped the list. It was never truer than of the Everly Brothers song they were playing.

> When I want you, in my arms
> When I want you, with all your charms
> Whenever I want you,
> All I have to do is Dream.

The first time he ever heard it, Jonathan felt this song had been written for him. It expressed his feelings for Jenny to a tee.

> Only trouble is, gee whiz
> I'm dreaming my life away.
> I need...

Silence. Then he heard the announcement.

"We interrupt this program to bring you a special bulletin from ABC radio".... Here is a special bulletin from Dallas, Texas.... Three shots were fired at President Kennedy's motorcade today in downtown Dallas, Texas."

The moment he heard it, thoughts of Jenny, the game, and the National Championship all vanished. They would not resurface until four, long, excruciating days later.

JENNY KISSED ME!

Jonathan hit the brakes without as much as a glance at the rear view mirror. He quickly wheeled his car around and headed back home. As soon as he pulled into the driveway, he got out and ran around to the back yard where he had just left his mother hanging clothes on the line.

"Mom, somebody just shot at President Kennedy in Dallas!"

"Oh no!" she gasped, putting her hand to her mouth. "Is he hurt?"

"They didn't say. All the radio said was there were shots fired."

They made their way into the living room and switched on the television. Standing silently, they watched. They were still in front of the TV set when Walter Cronkite told the nation the fateful news. Based on the newsman's somber countenance, Jonathan expected the worst. ***"Here is a bulletin: CBS news from Dallas, Texas. A flash..., apparently official."*** Cronkite removed his glasses and continued, ***"President Kennedy died at 1 p.m. Central Standard Time...."***

Jonathan and his mother looked at one another in disbelief. No words were exchanged. They hugged.

Jonathan had known only three presidents in his lifetime. Two of them, Truman and Eisenhower, were well along in years when they occupied the oval office. To him, they were more like grandfather figures. Kennedy was different. He was inaugurated at the age of forty-three, the second youngest ever to be elected to the presidency. His youth and vitality, along with the attractiveness of an even younger wife, captured the fascination of young people. It was inconceivable to Jonathan that Kennedy was dead. Then the coincidences struck him: Lyndon Johnson, the man to succeed Kennedy, graduated from Southwest Texas State, the university he attended. Walter Cronkite was once a student at the University of Texas, where Jenny was in school. These trivial facts swirled in his mind.

The days that followed were surreal. They seemed more dream than reality, but this dream was a nightmare. He watched, along with millions, the excruciating scenes on television: the flag-covered casket, the drums and bagpipes, the accused assassin being shot, and the president's widow holding the hands of her two young children. He knew the sights and sounds which unfolded before him would be forever etched in his memory.

The deluge of agonizing images plunged Jonathan into a depression he had not known since his father's death. Thoughts of the upcoming football game and seeing Jenny again were completely forgotten during those four long days.

Tuesday morning brought a change when Jonathan read a local newspaper article which considered whether the game ought to be played or canceled in deference to the deceased president. Pondering the issue, Jonathan came down on the side of going through with the contest as scheduled. Strangely, the matter of seeing Jenny was not a factor in his thinking. He believed the country needed a respite from the shock and grief of the last several days. However, once the decision was made to play on Thanksgiving Day,

JENNY KISSED ME!

Jonathan's thoughts relentlessly returned to his secret love.

Game day arrived. A bleary-eyed Jonathan looked into the mirror while he shaved that morning. Thoughts of Jenny had limited him to three hours sleep. On his way to pick up his friend, Jonathan decided to ask Tollie to take the wheel.

The drive to College Station took less than two hours, but it couldn't pass fast enough. Knowing that Jenny waited at destination's end, Jonathan could not contain his emotions. By the time he and Tollie left the city limits of San Marcos, his anticipation gauge had already pegged out. To speed up the time, he talked nonstop about the game and its magnitude.

"Number one in the nation, national championship, undefeated. It's all on the line."

Tollie interrupted, "This one's money in the bank."

Jonathan continued. "I wasn't concerned at first, but—"

Tollie interrupted again, "What are you bothered about? You think preoccupation with the president's death might have affected preparation?"

"You bet I do, but there's more to it than that."

"Let's hear it."

"You remember two years ago when Texas played TCU?"

"I'd rather not."

"Well that figures. We were undefeated then too. It was the next to the last game of the season, and we were twenty-five point favorites on our own field. We lost."

"Yeah, but those were the Frogs and these are the Aggies. No sweat."

Tollie was wrong. Many longhorn fans soaked their burnt orange apparel with perspiration before the game was history.

Jonathan's worries began shortly after he found his seat and saw the horrendous condition of the playing field. It was wet and muddy. He was immediately suspicious. Though it had rained some, it seemed to him more than God had watered the field. He nudged Tollie. "Check out that mess down there. It looks like a pigsty. That'll neutralize our speed advantage."

Tollie grinned and said, "No sweat."

Tollie's words never registered, and the condition of the field was forgotten, overpowered by the sudden appearance of who was on the sidelines—the Longhorn cheerleaders. Jonathan instantly spotted Jenny. It was easy. She was by far the prettiest one. He was astonished. *She's even more beautiful.* Then he challenged his own observation, *How can that be? You can't improve on a ten... Oh Jenny, if we could just talk again.*

For three quarters, Jonathan watched with mixed emotions. The view on the sidelines was wonderful; the view on the field was painful. The underdog Texas A&M team was outplaying his Longhorns. Entering the fourth quarter, they were in the lead. Tollie was no longer grinning. He was silent as a tomb. The sight would have been unbearable had it not been for the view on the sidelines. It was pure rapture to gaze upon Jenny's stunning face. Then midway through the fourth quarter, his emotions were no longer mixed. They all headed south.

"I've noticed those binoculars aren't always trained on the game," Tollie said.

"Yeah, just been checking out the Texas cheerleaders," Jonathan replied.

"You mean Jenny?"

"Yep, class of '60. We're proud of her, right?"

"You know, she is *engaged*, don't you?"

Jonathan's heart stopped. He said nothing as he continued to look through his binoculars, moving them away from Jenny and over to the field of play. A moment later he managed a forced response, "No, I didn't."

"Some rich frat rat from Dallas," Tollie said. "She always was out of our league."

Jonathan didn't comment. He would have left right then if he hadn't been with Tollie. But he continued to watch the remainder of the game through the field glasses, hiding his eyes from his friend lest his secret be revealed. He never again directed the binoculars toward Jenny.

When a final Texas drive was halted by an Aggie interception, all Longhorn hopes seemed doomed. For a few seconds, any possibility of a victory seemed irretrievably lost. Then for some inexplicable reason, the Aggie defender, who made the pick, attempted to lateral the football. A fumble.

Texas recovered.

Tollie leaped to his feet in jubilation! As he sat back down, he whispered in Jonathan's ear, softly so that none of the enemy could hear, "Did you see what that Aggie *did*?"

Jonathan saw it, but it didn't connect.

Texas, given new life by virtue of the Aggie gift, scored the winning touchdown with scarcely over a minute left to play. The loyal Texas fandom in attendance erupted in hysteria, jumping up and down, shouting, and flashing the Hook'em Horns sign. In the entire stadium, there was probably only one orange clad person who remained seated. It was Jonathan, staring ahead, the binoculars in his lap. He watched the final minutes in a daze, oblivious to the action on the field. His mind was far off, filled with the same anguish he had experienced years before, in the aftermath of revealing his heart to Jenny in the poem.

On their way to exit Kyle Field, Tollie was puzzled by Jonathan's lack of exuberance. "What's wrong with you, Kaelin?" Tollie poked him with his elbow. "We're going to be National Champs!"

Jonathan mumbled, "It was too close for comfort. It'll hit me later. I'll get into the mood…."

But his mood did not change. Even though Texas won their first football National Championship, the gloom did not go away. The nation had lost a president, and Jonathan had lost Jenny *forever.*

TEN

The Letter

Two months later in early January 1964, Jenny reached into the mailbox at her parents' home and clasped half a dozen envelopes. She glanced at the one on the top, addressed to her mother. It brought tears to her eyes. There was no reason to sift through the rest. They would all be addressed the same—all cards and letters of condolence. They had poured in for several days now since the death of her father.

Jenny paused outside the front door and welcomed the entrance of a happier memory when she was a little girl, sitting at the kitchen table with her mom, dad, and brother...

It was around noon and she was enjoying a treat not available to most of her school mates. The proximity of the elementary school allowed her to come home for lunch. Ross Nichols, her father, was in the insurance business and normally planned his lunch hour to be with his family.

While they ate they'd often hear a familiar sound come from the place where she now stood. It was the sound made by the postman as he dropped the day's mail in the box outside their front door. Jenny's face would light up. "May I be excused?" Her parents would nod, and she would get up and race to the front door. Then, standing on tiptoes, she would reach up into the mailbox and retrieve what Mr. Flowers had placed there. Dashing back into the house, she would hand the contents to her father.

"Thank you, Little Bit," he would say as he distributed the mail between him and Jenny's mom. Only two or three times had there ever been a card or letter for Jenny. It didn't matter; she enjoyed the ritual of listening for the sound of the postman on the porch and bringing the mail to her father. It made her feel important, somehow...

Revisiting the scene brought a pool of tears. She had been at home for ten days now—one of her longer stays during the three and a half years since she pulled out of the driveway in her packed 1957 turquoise and white Chevrolet and headed to Austin. The most traumatic experience of her twenty-one years brought her home for this extended stay. Its intrusion had come at a time of merriment.

Jenny and Teller, her fiancé, had invited some friends over to her apartment to welcome in the New Year. The next day, Texas played Navy in the Cotton Bowl. It would be her last game as a Texas cheerleader. The Longhorns had already been crowned national champion by virtue of their perfect regular season record, but there was still the matter of playing the midshipman on New Years' Day in Dallas.

Navy, led by Heisman trophy winner Roger Staubach, was just behind them in the polls, so it would be number one against number two. Jenny could not have special ordered a more exciting finale to her cheerleading years. She planned to leave Austin for the drive to "Big D" before the sun came up. Sleep would be minimal, but she knew that adrenalin would provide sufficient fuel for the trip and the game to follow.

It was a journey Jenny would never make. The phone rang a few minutes after the midnight eruption. Shouts of revelry were still in the air, along with the poppity-pop-pop of firecrackers in the street outside. Jenny assumed the ringing telephone was a friend calling. She anticipated three words—"Happy New Year!" Instead, when she picked up the phone there was silence, though it was clear someone was on the other end of the line.

Intuitively, Jenny's throat and stomach tightened, sensing bad news of some sort. Her mother's sobbing voice informed her that her father had just been rushed to the hospital. Words that followed, broken with emotion, were barely coherent.

Jenny said, "Mom, I'm on my way. I'll see you at the hospital. Don't worry. Daddy will be okay. He's always been healthy."

But Jenny's father was not okay. He had suffered a massive stroke. By the time Jenny and a friend made the fifty minute drive to the hospital in San Marcos, he had expired.

Ross Nichols demise was Jenny's first real encounter with death. She vaguely remembered her great-grandmother's funeral, which happened when she was six. Her granny had died in her late eighties—when death is supposed to come. For her father, who was only fifty years of age, it had arrived early, unexpectedly, and—it seemed—unfairly. The pain of its untimeliness was compounded by thoughts of what was ahead.

Jenny had anticipated two celebrations in the coming months, both among life's happiest occasions. She could not imagine her father not being there for either of them. First, her college graduation was in May. For as long as she could remember, Ross Nichols had planned for both of his children to go to college. Jenny, the oldest, would lead the way.

Then soon after graduation, a June wedding was planned. Her dad was supposed to walk her down the aisle, and give her in marriage. She had pictured it in her mind so many times. He would be in his tuxedo, smiling at her, just as he did when she was a little girl, and he came into her bedroom to kiss her good night. Jenny anguished over why her family had been robbed of the happiness of these special occasions—on the very threshold of their celebration.

Jenny was close to both of her parents. She and her mom had become closer in recent years, as they shared more as woman to woman. It was different with her father. They had always been close. She was Daddy's girl.

She was five years old the first time she remembered hearing the expression. Her father and a

JENNY KISSED ME!

neighbor were conversing across the chain link fence while Jenny played in the backyard. "Ross, I see you've got yourself a real daddy's girl." Jenny was not sure what it meant, but it made her proud. It was the reason she continued to call him "Daddy," even though many of her friends switched to the more common "Dad" when they got to be teenagers. The name "Daddy" brought back memories of a little girl, a backyard fence, and a beaming father. She had never forgotten the look that day on her father's face.

Ross Nichols and his daughter were two peas in a pod. Jenny's mom was an introvert, but Jenny possessed the outgoing extrovert personality of her dad. They both loved being around people, the more the merrier. Wherever they were, you expected to hear lively conversation and more than a sprinkling of laughter. They even grinned alike. She could hear the words now, *"Look at that grin. Tell me that's not Ross Nichols' daughter."*

Jenny and her dad had continued to be close even while she was away at college. Geography could not change that. He was in Austin for business twice a month and would inevitably meet her for lunch—just the two of them. Later they added Jenny's friends, and throughout the last year Teller frequently met with them. It seemed to her like yesterday, although it was almost a month since one of those occasions together. It was during fall semester finals, the last time.

ৡৡৡ

A week had passed since the funeral. The minister, a close friend of her father's, had delivered a beautiful eulogy in a filled church. He had mentioned many of her father's endearing qualities—including the grin. Jenny appreciated his words, but when she walked out of the church, she knew it would be a while before she exhibited that shared characteristic.

Her mother had leaned heavily on Jenny throughout the days following her father's death. Adjusting to life without her husband seemed to leave her at loose ends. A few days after the funeral, while they sat on the couch and shared memories of her dad, Jenny had offered a suggestion. "Mom, I only need six hours to graduate, and I could pick those up in the summer. Wouldn't you like me to stay home this semester so I can be here with you?"

Her mother had reached over and patted Jenny's hand. "Thank you, Sweet, but I want you to go back for the spring semester. Your Daddy would want you to graduate with your class in May. You know how important it was to him. Besides, I've got Carol and Mark next door if I need anything, and there are my church friends." Then she had leaned over and kissed Jenny on the cheek. "I'm going to be all right."

Her mom had said the right words, but Jenny knew they lacked the power of conviction. In truth, Nancy Nichols was not all right. She frequently retired to the bedroom, and her returns left no doubt as to the reason for those withdrawals. Nancy's clear green eyes took on a permanent redness. Furthermore, the high energy level for which she was known had dissipated. Ordinarily, she rarely sat during the normal course of a day, perpetually busying herself with activities both inside and outside of the home. Now she spent hours sitting at the kitchen table, hands folded, staring off into space. That's what she was doing while Jenny was on the porch holding the condolence cards and remembering.

❧❧❧

Jenny's mother looked up from the table as her daughter approached with mail in hand. Receiving it, she sorted through the envelopes at a slow pace while Jenny headed upstairs toward her bedroom.

"Jenny, one of these cards is addressed to you."

Assuming it was a sympathy card from a friend, she shouted back, "I'll get it later, Mom."

"Jenny, do you know someone who lives on Field Street? There's no name, just an address."

Quickly retracing her steps back to the kitchen, Jenny answered while reaching for the card, "Yes, there was someone in my class who lived on Field Street."

She hastily retreated to her room, but she did not rush to open the envelope. Instead she stared at the address on the upper left hand corner, as a smile began to build. For the first time since that phone call on New Year's Eve, her smile was not forced. *Jonathan...it's been a long time.*

The card was nice, but the envelope contained more. Inside was a folded letter.

> *Dear Jenny,*
> *I'm so sorry to hear about your dad. I apologize for not making it to the funeral. I*

was out of town for the holidays and didn't hear about it until I returned.

Jenny, I don't know whether I ever told you this, but I lost my father when I was only fourteen. The memory of when I first heard the news is still vivid in my mind, so I know the pain you're going through. Even so, I can offer you some good news, from my own experience. I have learned as time goes by the pain will lessen, but your memories will grow stronger and even more precious. Time will heal.

Remember those conversations we shared our senior year, before and after the classes we had together. You have probably forgotten this, but one time you told me all about your dad (or as you called him, Daddy). You mentioned what a good man he was, how much alike the two of you were, and what an impact he had on your life. Jenny, if what I saw in you is your father's influence, he really was a wonderful man.

You know me and poetry. I couldn't find a poem that exactly expressed my feelings. So, I took the liberty to write one for you. I'm a novice at this, but it comes from my heart.

Jenny, your dad died too young, as did mine. These thoughts are to remind you that it's not the quantity of our years that ultimately matters, but the quality of our lives. And don't forget, your dad lives on, in you.

JENNY KISSED ME!

A life lived in abundance of years
May or not have an influence in time.
Though the man of virtue, touching lives
on his way
Although brief, has affect quite sublime.

Think not then of grief, though the days
went so fast
And the laughter slipped quickly away.
For that which will last and grow
stronger each day
Are memories that years can't allay.

Jonathan

P.S. Jenny, I heard about your engagement. I wish you the very best in your marriage. You will always be my favorite senior girl, and I desire your happiness more than anyone I know.

She looked up from the page, and spoke the words softly to the solitude of her room. "Jonathan, this is so much like you."

Jenny sat down in the chair by her window and looked outside, contemplating the letter and the renewed memories of Jonathan it had inspired. Finally, she took a deep breath and stood up. There were tears in her eyes. She needed time to be alone and think. So her mom would not see the tears, she moved quietly down the stairs to the front hall. Opening the door, she raised her voice. "Mom I'm going for a walk. I'll be back shortly."

Jenny didn't return as early as she anticipated. She was gone for almost an hour. The burden, which had induced her decision to take a walk, seemed to grow heavier with each step. For the first time since the foreboding New Years' Eve call, thoughts of her father receded, replaced by images of two other men.

One was Jonathan. The letter from him rekindled memories and feelings from the past. The other man was the person she was due to marry in five months. The persistent picture that arose in her mind was one of marked contrast—two young men, so different, yet each so important to her.

Doubts enveloped her thoughts of Teller. They had been there for some time but had grown more pronounced within the last year. Still, whenever they surfaced she had managed to ignore them. Now she could no longer do that, not with Jonathan's reemergence. Thoughts of him invited comparisons with her fiancé and only magnified the uncertainties about her approaching marriage.

Jonathan's thoughtfulness stood in stark relief to the insensitivity of her fiancé, which had manifested itself more than a few times during their three years together. One occasion during the previous fall semester had even caused her to temporarily break up with Teller. The incident involved her roommate Linda, who had steadily dated a boy since their sophomore year in high school. Their relationship continued while he was at Texas Tech, and they had planned to marry following graduation…

One day, Jenny found Linda crying, with a Dear John letter lying on the floor near her bed. Later in the afternoon Jenny called Teller.

"Tel, I need to stay in tonight."

"What's wrong?"

"Linda just got a letter from Sal. He broke off their engagement. It was a total shock. She's been crying since I came home from class. I'm going to stay with her."

"What about the movie?"

"We'll catch it later. Linda needs somebody with her right now."

"She'll get over it, Jenny. These things happen all the time. She probably needs some time by herself."

"Tel, she's my friend. I'm sorry, but I need to be with her. Do you understand?"

There was no answer, just the click of a receiver.

When morning came, Teller wasn't waiting for her at the place on campus where they normally met. He was usually there, and they would walk to Friday morning classes together. Jenny didn't think much about it, assuming that he probably overslept. She learned differently when he called her later that afternoon.

"Did you miss me this morning?" he asked.

"Yes, did you forget to set your alarm?"

"No. I didn't appreciate you breaking our date last night. Now you know how it feels."

Jenny was stunned. For a moment there was silence. Then the measured words came. "You mean you didn't meet me because you wanted to punish me for sympathizing with a friend?"

"Well forget it," Teller snapped back. "What time do you want me to pick you up tonight?"

Seconds ticked away. Jenny could sense her face turning red as a hot surge of resentment engulfed her. Fully realizing the import of the words she was about to speak, she calmly told Teller, "I don't want you to pick me up this evening. I think it would be good for us not to see each other for a while." Jenny returned the phone to the receiver without waiting for a response.

The next three days were difficult for Jenny. Weighing the pros and cons of her relationship with Teller sapped her usual energy. Her body felt tired and her appetite disappeared. She had an almost constant headache. Since the two had been practically inseparable from the time of their freshman year, loneliness overwhelmed her. However, in her solitude she began to picture her boyfriend more objectively, and doubts crept in. But that all changed on the fourth day when Teller caught her on the way to class. He brought a bundle of apologies, and a surprise—an engagement ring.

Jenny wasn't the first of her company of friends to receive such a gift. But never had she seen a diamond of such size. The effect on her senses was immediate and transforming. Her missing energies returned and the headache vanished. Under the spell of the ring's brilliance and sparkle, all was forgotten as she flew into Teller's arms. The next day the two began making wedding plans ...

JENNY KISSED ME!

As Jenny continued walking in the neighborhood, a more recent example of Teller's thoughtlessness came to mind. It had happened New Year's Eve at the worst possible time—when Jenny's mother called after rushing her dad to the hospital…

As Jenny told her fiancé about it, her eyes filled with tears. "Tel, it's serious. Mother is crying…she can't even talk."

A friend standing nearby immediately embraced her. Teller just stood there, seemingly preoccupied. He finally said. "I'm sure he'll be okay. Why don't you drive on down to the hospital? I'll stay here. It wouldn't be very hospitable to break up the party this early."

Jenny's friend focused an incredulous stare at Teller, aghast at what she heard. She quickly offered her assistance.

"Jenny, I'll drive you to San Marcos."

Later when Jenny called to inform her fiancé that her father had died, he said, "I'm so sorry to hear that." Then he rushed to add, "We're not going to postpone the wedding, are we?" Jenny was speechless, her spirit crushed by his lack of feeling. There was a moment of silence during which her soul silently screamed. *Don't you understand? My father has just died!*

Then her thoughts formed and her words came out curtly, "I don't want to talk about that now, Tel." As her voice choked with emotion, she sobbed, "Daddy's gone."

When Teller finally showed up at the house, he brought hugs, kisses, and the usual excuses, but this time the hurt remained…

Thomas Allen

৵৵৵

As Jenny returned home from her walk and opened the front door, she was irresistibly drawn to a small room in the rear of the house. She had not entered it since her father's death. It was his study. Memories returned as she looked about the room—the books, the file cabinets, the pictures, and the desk. She walked over and sat down in the chair where he always sat. She picked up the family picture on his desk. Her eyes rested on the tall figure in the back, and she sighed, determined to hold back the tears.

How many times as a little girl and later a teenager she had visited him here in this very room to share the events of the school day. She talked of people—friends, teachers, even boyfriends. Then there had been those occasions of a problem too big to wrap her head around. Her father's perception spotted those moments as soon as she entered his room. He'd stop whatever he was doing and give her his undivided attention. *Daddy was a grand listener*. In those sessions he talked very little, instead he listened and asked questions. Most of the time, before she left, she had solved the problem herself.

She returned the picture to the desk and leaned back in his chair. *Oh, Daddy, I need you.* A tear fell. *I wish I knew what you thought.*

When Jenny went up to her room, she walked over to the dresser and held her hand under the lamp. She stared at the big engagement ring. It didn't seem so brilliant now. A question lay heavily on her mind—*What kind of man am I marrying?*

JENNY KISSED ME!

She stooped down to open the bottom drawer of the chest-of-drawers. It was cluttered with high school pictures and keepsakes. Shuffling past the party invitations, homecoming ribbons, the football and prom programs, she found a shoebox filled with pictures she had not seen since she left for college. She lifted the lid.

There on the top where she had placed it was Jonathan's school picture. Holding it in her hand, she sat down on the bed as memories emanated from the image. She stared at it, motionless, as a wave of sadness came over her.

Jonathan, how could I have forgotten...? Jenny wiped her eyes.

Gradually, her countenance softened as thoughts of special times flashed by—the poem, classes they shared, the kiss in the library, the time they danced, and graduation night when they looked into each other's eyes the last time. Her thoughts lingered and hours went by.

Now in the midst of her greatest loss, life thrust a momentous decision upon her. The emotional turmoil it fostered pulled at her as the night stretched on.

Not yet ready to sleep, Jenny walked into the hall. It was dark except for a small night light. The door to her mother's room was closed, so Jenny tiptoed past. Her mom went to bed earlier now; sleep provided a much-needed reprieve from the emotional drain.

Jenny went downstairs and slid open the glass door to the patio. As she stepped outside, an unusually warm January night greeted her. She sat down on a lounge chair and gazed up at the star splashed sky. Soon a decision started to clarify.

Pragmatically, the choice was an easy one. Teller's family was wealthy, and he was destined to follow suit. Marrying him meant security. They would have the best home, probably more than one, emulating his parents who resided in exclusive North Dallas while maintaining a vacation home on the Texas coast. They would socialize with the right people, and their children would go to the best schools. Marrying Teller would mean fulfilling the American dream. It was, after all, the expected and logical step to take.

But, there was the *other* dream, the unpractical persistent one, first fashioned in her imagination by that new boy at school who spoke the words, "...the heart that has truly loved never forgets, but as truly loves on to the close...."

With Teller, she would have all the trappings of the good life. But would she have the heart-felt assurance Jonathan promised in his poem so many years ago?

As the hours ticked away, she anguished over the toll that the last three years had taken on her heart, silencing its whisperings. Now at home again, with the letter and its poem in her hand, the repressed longings of her heart returned. *When the night was darkest, Jonathan came back into my life and brought me light.* Finally exhausted, she fell asleep on the recliner, clutching the letter.

When Jenny awoke at dawn, her eyes fell immediately on the letter, now lying on her lap. As she touched it, she realized that sometime during the night while she was asleep, her heart won the battle.

Folding the letter and lightly kissing it, she walked quietly back into the house. Once in her room, she placed the letter and his photo back in the shoebox—right on top—and whispered, "Jonathan, I'll never forget…never again."

There was an indescribable exhilaration, a new lightness in her mood as she got ready that morning. The idea she might see Jonathan for the first time in over three years filled her with anticipation.

Right after breakfast, I'll call him. Before she left her room, she took off her engagement ring and placed it in her jewelry box. *I don't want him to see this when I walk up to him... when I run up to him.* She smiled and spoke out loud, "This time I *will* tell him my heart."

Jenny left her room, bolted down the stairs, covering the last step in a single stride. As she entered the kitchen, she immediately noticed a difference in her mother. Instead of sitting, she was busy at the stove and smiled as her daughter came into the room. Encouraged by her mother's changed demeanor, Jenny cheerfully kissed her cheek and sat down at the breakfast table.

Her mother spoke first. "Darling, I realized something last night. For your Daddy's sake we both need to be happy, as happy as he was with your approaching graduation and wedding. So I'm all cried out for now."

As her mom continued, Jenny's heart shattered.

"Daddy was so proud of the man you're going to marry, because more than anything else he wanted a son-in-law who could take good care of his little girl. He often said 'That guy is going places.' Your Daddy died happy knowing Teller is going to be your husband."

Jenny was speechless.

"What's wrong, darling? Is it talking about your father? I know it hurts, because he's not going to be at the wedding to give you away."

Jenny had heard only a few of the words. Most of them were silenced by, "*Daddy was so proud of the man you're going to marry...*," which pierced her soul like a dagger.

"Jenny, you want me to make you some breakfast?"

Jenny managed to shake her head as she left the table. She went directly to her room and closed the door, burying her head in a pillow to hide the sound.

An hour later, she came out of her room. Jenny now knew what her father thought and what she had to do. She would marry Teller. It would honor her dad and please her mom.

Walking back through the kitchen, she hugged her mother and forced a smile. "Mom, I've got some things to do. I'll be back in a bit."

When Jenny drove out of their driveway, she didn't know where she was going. She just felt compelled to get away. But she soon found herself on the way to Jonathan's house. As she approached Field Street she whispered, "Jonathan please be there, please be in the yard."

He was not there. She had no idea what she would have done if he had been. She just needed to see him—one more time.

Five minutes later, she drove by again. Still there was no Jonathan.

She drove by Sandra's house, through familiar parts of town, and then headed back to Jonathan's

JENNY KISSED ME!

house a third time. Just before she turned onto his block, she silenced the volume on the radio. As she passed his home, she finally whispered the words, longed stored in her heart, "Jonathan…I love you…"

ೞೞೞ

As glimmers of light peeked through the plane's window, Jenny lifted the shade, anticipating clouds and sea below. Instead she saw the approach of a large city. It was Rome. Arrival came earlier than expected. She had been so consumed with thoughts of Jonathan; she hadn't heard the announcement of the plane's approach.

Now, it was time to put away memories of the boy she once loved. But one scene lingered—the one with her mother that morning. She shook her head, astonished at how a few words spoken at the breakfast table had so altered the course of her life.

ELEVEN

Veiled Reunion

John and Jenny's planes arrived in Rome only hours apart. They had never imagined, when they walked away from each other graduation night 1960, it would be forty years and five thousand miles away before they would meet again.

The impossibility of recapturing the past was immortalized in Thomas Wolfe's bestselling 1940's novel, *You Can't Go Home Again*. The effect of time upon change gives ample testimony to the author's truism. The passing of four decades brought outward changes to John and Jenny that masked any recognition of one another. But matters of the heart are not governed by time. The words from the poem Jonathan had recited to Jenny in high school—"the heart that has truly loved, never forgets"—was still alive within both of them. Old feelings had been awakened by memories on the flight over, and when the planes touched Italian soil, a seed had been planted.

Although John and Jenny happened to be part of the same tour group, they didn't meet until the third day. The first two days in the city had not gone well for either of them, especially John.

His experiences were bittersweet, with memories of Claire overwhelmed by the reality that she was not there to share them. Near the end of the first day, he questioned his own sanity in making the trip. In his hotel room that evening, John became so despondent he started to call his daughter and tell her he planned to head home on the next available flight. However, realizing the worry it would cause Harper, he dismissed the impulse. Besides, he knew that the same loneliness awaited him across the Atlantic—there would be no Claire.

Jenny's first two days held her interest, but they didn't offer the excitement she had imagined. Something was wrong. While she observed the lighthearted banter, smiles, and exchanged looks of Bud and Kay, her companions on the flight over, she realized what was missing. Sandra had been right. In spite of her denial, Jenny still longed for someone to love. Here she was, captivated by the sights and sounds of the most romantic city in the world, and no special person to share it with.

During this time, John and Jenny didn't take notice of one another, at least not more than a passing glance.

As the second day drew to a close, something happened that not only set the stage for their meeting, but ultimately made possible John and Jenny's recognition of each other.

Each evening the tour group dined at a nice restaurant. Carlita, their perky Italian tour guide, encouraged socializing, and suggested that the travelers eat with different people each evening for the first few days. That suggestion brought John into the company of Bud and Kay, the Indiana couple. Their table was quickly filled with lively discussion on a variety of topics and interests. Before the evening ended, they were reminded of the old maxim: "It's a small world." Their conversation revealed the possibility that the three of them might have crossed paths before, years ago. Responding to an inquiry about his roots, John revealed he had not always lived in Arizona but grew up in a small Texas town called San Marcos.

Kay lit up. "We've been there—on vacation in the late fifties."

"It was 1958," Bud suggested.

"No," Kay corrected. "It was the summer of 1959."

Bud shook his head and pointed his thumb at his wife, sitting to the right of him. "She's right. I know that because she's always right about these things." Then he added with a tone of resignation, "That's what makes it so irritating." He smiled.

As the conversation unfolded, John entertained the thought that maybe he had been their Wonder Cave tour guide. He worked there that summer. The Garners were so likable and easy to be around that John heard himself laughing quite frequently—something he had done little of since his wife's death. He even talked about Claire. As it turned out, meeting the couple was the link to his secret love of long ago. They met the very next day.

ৡ৵ৡ৵ৡ৵

John and Jenny met at the famous Spanish Steps. As providence would have it, a poet brought them together.

Carlita completed her lecture on the history of the steps—the longest and widest staircase in Europe. Afterwards, she gave the group time to take pictures and to walk down to the Piazza di Spagna, a plaza at the base of the steps. Jenny was talking to Kay when Bud noticed John standing at the bottom of the steps, looking back at a pink building on his right.

"Kay, look, there's John. Let's see what he's up to."

"Elaine, have you met John?" Kay asked.

"No, I haven't," she said, as she looked over and saw an attractive man she had noticed walking by her table at breakfast.

"He's a college professor from Arizona." Kay raised her voice. "Quite interesting. He ate dinner at our table last night." She grabbed Jenny's arm. "Let's go, I'll introduce you."

The two walked over to meet him, and Bud followed. Kay initiated the introduction. "John," she said, "let me introduce you to Elaine Ames. She came over on our flight. Elaine, this is John...." Kay hesitated. "I'm sorry, I forgot your—"

"That's okay, most people do," he said. "It's Kaelin. Happy meeting you, Elaine."

Elaine extended her hand. "Hi! John, it's nice to meet you."

John reacted, and offered his hand in response. Halfway through the motion, he paused, his hand freezing in mid-air several inches from Jenny's. Their eyes met and something happened.

Bud noticed John's hesitation and broke the silence. "What's the matter? Got your mind on something else?"

John regained his composure. "I'm sorry, you did say Elaine?"

"Yes."

Then John clasped her hand. "It's nice to meet you, Elaine. I did have my mind on something else. You know, the absent minded professor thing."

Bud said. "I noticed you looking at something when we walked up. Kay was curious."

"Yes, see the second floor of that building," John said. "It's where the great romantic poet Keats died."

"Really?" said Kay. "Is there a story to it?"

"Yeah, there is," John said. "But are you sure you want to get me started on this?" He glanced at Elaine. "A lot of folks find this stuff boring, you know."

Jenny acknowledged his gaze with raised eyebrows and said, "I'm for sure not one of them. I'd like to hear it."

"Well, it doesn't hurt to check, because to tell you the truth, I can't exactly say students beat the door down to get into my classroom."

"I can understand that." Bud interjected caustically.

John laughed and spread out his hands. "See what I mean."

"Ignore him," Kay said.

"Please go on." Jenny asked.

"Alright, but you can leave any time you like." He grinned as he began his spiel. "Keats came here from England, hoping to improve his health. He suffered from tuberculosis or consumption, as they called it back then. He thought the warmer climate in Rome would be healthier. He lived there on the second story with a painter, Joseph Severn, who arrived with him on the boat."

"Do you know what year that was?" Kay asked. "Dates connect with me; they give me a historical context."

"Me too." Bud said.

John chuckled. "Yeah, I can tell that." Turning to Kay he continued. "They arrived here in November of 1820. Three months later Keats died. Since Severn took care of him, he's the source for almost all of the information we have about the poet's last days. Severn even sketched Keats while he slept, less than a month prior to his death. It's the last portrait of him."

"Did they take him home to England for burial?" Jenny asked.

"No, he's buried in the Protestant cemetery here, a beautiful place. Very tranquil. You're almost unaware that Rome surrounds it."

John noticed the two women seemed interested. Meanwhile, Bud was glancing at a brochure on the coliseum.

"Are you curious about the rest of the story?" John asked.

"Yes, please, go on," Jenny encouraged.

"You may recall that Keats was a young man when he died, a mere twenty-five. He asked Severn to have these words inscribed on his tombstone: 'Here Lies One Whose Name Was Writ In Water.' How's that for an epitaph. Well, Severn lived almost another sixty years, but he's buried here in the same cemetery beside Keats."

Kay leaned toward Jenny and whispered, "I told you he was interesting."

Jenny didn't respond to Kay's statement because her mind had drifted. If she had, it would have been an enthusiastic nod. But her thoughts were focused instead on her reaction to the man himself. Earlier, she had experienced an immediate comfort in his presence, like she knew him. Jenny was normally at ease making new friends, but she couldn't recall anything quite like this.

John's words jarred her back into the moment.

"Now, ladies, are you ready for the romantic stuff?"

"Please," Kay encouraged, while Bud rolled his eyes.

"Buried with Keats is a letter from his true love and a lock of her hair. That was also in his final request to Severn."

"Who was she?" Jenny spoke with excitement. Then embarrassed at her own enthusiasm, she changed her tone to sound more casual, "I'd like to hear the whole story."

"Well, Keats was in love with a woman named Fanny Browne. They were secretly engaged. He wrote her many love letters."

"And they never married?" Jenny asked.

"No, they didn't. It was a matter of finances plus his bad health. Keats was not a successful poet during his lifetime. His fame came years later. At one time, he wrote to Fanny and told her she was free to break their engagement, but she didn't comply. Severn later believed that Keats' fatal illness was as much a result of his unfulfilled love life, as the consumption itself."

Bud had listened until now. "You're telling us he died of a broken heart, right?"

"Do I detect a tinge of cynicism?" John asked.

Kay glared at her husband over her glasses. Then she turned to John. "Please go on. Pretend he's not here. What happened to Fanny after Keats died? Do we know?"

"Well, after some time, she married and had several children. She died over forty years after Keats."

"Wouldn't you love to read those love letters?" Jenny said, mainly to herself.

"You can." John said. "For Keats' devotees, this is perhaps the most intriguing aspect of their relationship. Fanny kept most of his letters. As her children got older, she told them about Keats and the letters, but she made them promise never to tell their father. I think it was about a decade after their parents' deaths when the kids auctioned off the letters. And they were eventually published."

"Sometimes the most romantic stories are the true ones." Jenny said.

For the first time since he extended his hand, once again their eyes met. "I think that's true much of the time. It was Elaine, right?"

Jenny nodded.

"Would you like to hear a line from one of his letters to Fanny?"

Bud responded with a quick rib, "If I told you how I feel about that offer, I'd face the ire of these two gals. So, by all means, go on." He looked at his watch. "You've got thirty seconds."

Before John could respond, Kay elbowed Bud. "Are you still here?" She gave him a gentle push and gestured toward the steps. "Why don't you go climb those…all the way back to the top."

John chuckled and continued. "Well, Keats wrote to Fanny about his restless, wandering mind. According to him, he had difficulty focusing on anything without being distracted. Being in Fanny's presence was the lone exception. He wrote, 'When you are in the room, you always concentrate my whole senses.'"

Kay turned to her husband. "Why don't you ever say anything like that to me?"

Bud looked up and shrugged his shoulders.

John laughed. "Bud, let's face it. If you are not into romance, you miss much of the mystique that is Rome."

"Way to go, John," Kay encouraged, "but he doesn't even know what the word means. If he had his wish we'd spend all three days at the coliseum."

"Alright, we'll dump the poetry," John looked over at the women and winked. "Bud, you've been pretty patient with us, except for a few smart cracks, so we'll change the subject."

JENNY KISSED ME!

"When my wife and I were here several years ago, we took a Rome Movie tour. I suspect they've filmed more movies on location in Rome than any other place in the world. Bud you look like a movie buff to me—with limitations."

"Yeah, westerns, war movies, and film 'noir,'" Bud said.

Kay smirked. "You noticed he left out romantic ones."

"Big surprise," John said. "Bud, there's a building you might be interested in." John pointed to a structure on his right about halfway up the stairs. "That apartment was featured in a movie that had Rome in its title. Ring a bell with anyone?" They all shook their heads. "It was *The Roman Spring of Mrs. Stone*. It was obscure, but did any of you see it?" Once more, they responded in the negative.

"It's based on a Tennessee Williams novella."

Jenny exhibited an obvious frown.

"Problem, Elaine?"

"His movies are real downers, at least the ones I've seen."

"I agree with you, but they're considered intellectually chic for the literary crowd, so I've gone to some." He shook his head. "Afterwards, I usually end up in a dark bar, somewhere in the seedy part of town, drinking cheap liquor and listening to Sinatra on the jukebox singing 'Give Me One for My Baby, (and One More for the Road.)'"

Bud said, "I could buy in to that."

Kay giggled, and then said with sarcasm, "I can just picture both of you."

John said, "Well, I thought those words might suggest a scene from one of Tennessee's movies."

There was a rare silence as they walked toward a fountain in the piazza to get a better view of the stairs. With the respite, Jenny had time to mentally respond to Kay's earlier assessment: *Yes*, she nodded to herself, *he is an interesting man.*

As John looked back up the Spanish Steps, he pointed to a spot and said, "Anyone remember a famous movie scene filmed there? Now, this one's a bit more upbeat that Tennessee's."

Jenny's eyes lit up, and John was quick to notice.

"Elaine, I think a light just went on."

"*Roman Holiday.*"

"Describe the scene?"

"Gregory Peck finds the princess, Audrey Hepburn, sitting on the steps, eating an ice cream cone."

"I'm impressed." He glanced at her.

"I saw it last week." Jenny smiled.

৩৩৩৩

John was back in his hotel room by four o'clock. It was two hours until the group assembled for the evening meal, so he stretched out on the bed to rest and reflect. About ten minutes later his phone rang. It was Harper.

"It's great to hear your voice, daughter."

"Yours too, Pop. I miss you and I envy you. I bet you're having a good time."

"I am, Harper. I met some interesting people from the tour group who are fun to be with."

"Where are they from?"

"Somewhere in the Midwest... I think Indiana. They're a nice couple." John proceeded to talk about the Garners and the sights they saw that day.

After John hung up the phone, he thought about how good it was to hear Harper's voice. The older she got the more she reminded him of her mother—it was her voice. She sounded so much like Claire, most people couldn't tell the difference.

John had caught himself during their conversation. He was about to tell his daughter about Elaine. However, the idea bothered him. While grieving Claire, it didn't seem right for him to talk about a single woman. John noticed she wasn't wearing a ring. The fact he even noticed it disturbed him. Then there was the most unsettling thought of all—the strange sensation he had earlier that morning when their eyes first met. He had covered himself, by attributing his reaction to some distracting thought, which was not the case and he knew it. Had he been candid and expressed himself he would have said, "You remind me of someone."

John shook his head as if to clear his thoughts. *The eyes are the same, but the name isn't. It's not Jenny. Just wishful thinking. That's what I get for spending a long plane ride obsessing over someone. What would be the odds—only in a movie.*

As John lay down on the bed again, he thought of the day's activities, which lay ahead. Each evening he had looked forward to the multi course dinners, but tonight his anticipation heightened as he thought about joining Bud and Kay again. *I hope Elaine will be there too.*

When his thoughts returned to the day's events, he pondered a surprise happening—how he had drawn attention to the romantic movie, *Roman Holiday*. Since Claire's' death, he had wanted nothing to do with the genre. There was too much pain. Their first movie together had been *Breakfast at Tiffany's*. From then on, romantic movies became a favorite with them. With the coming of videocassette recorders and movie rentals, opportunities to enjoy a good one accelerated. He and Claire would watch a great love story—bowl of popcorn in-between—over and over again. In time they knew every scene and sometimes every line. Quotes from movies which would crop up in their daily conversation when the occasion fit were often topped off with a kiss. But several weeks after Claire's death, he separated the love stories from his video library and, with eyes blurry from tears, put them out of sight in the back of the hall closet.

A motor scooter horn beeped outside the window and broke his reverie, yanking his attention back to the events of the evening. After dinner, the tour group was going to Trevi, the most famous of the many fountains of Rome. It was the setting for *Three Coins in the Fountain,* a movie about some American girls who throw coins into the fountain and make wishes to someday return to Rome. He and Claire had watched the movie prior to their vacation in Italy. Imitating the action of the girls, they both made their wishes and

JENNY KISSED ME!

tossed their coins into the fountain's pool. John replayed the scene in his mind...

Claire spoke first. "I'll tell you my wish if you'll tell me yours."

John held up four fingers. "My wish is that I'll be here for our fortieth anniversary."

"Me too," Claire said. "Can we fly over together?"

"If you behave yourself."

Then they kissed...

John got up from the bed, splashed water on his face, combed his hair, and started downstairs.

While he walked to the bus for the ride to the restaurant, he was still recalling the events of that trip, when he heard a voice behind him. He turned and saw Elaine approaching, so he waited for her to catch up.

"John, I wanted to tell you how much I enjoyed hearing you talk about Keats today. Thanks for sharing his story. It's the most memorable thing I heard all day."

"I hope I didn't sound too much like a professor."

"Not at all. Anytime you want to share your expertise, I'm an eager listener."

"Apparently you enjoy poetry. Have you read much of it?"

"Not like you, but I did minor in English Lit. I became interested years ago in high school, when I knew a boy who loved poetry."

"A long forgotten love, as the poets would say." John teased.

"No," Jenny answered softly, "more of a secret one."

175

When they arrived at the restaurant, John did share the evening meal with Bud and Kay. And his wish came true. Elaine was also at the table.

֍֍֍

Trevi was very crowded when they arrived after dinner. People were talking, laughing, taking photos, tossing coins into the waters, and kissing. Jenny handed her camera to John. "I need a picture of the three of us in front of the fountain. When I get home, I'm going to be talking about these two characters I met on the trip, and I want pictures to prove they exist. Would you mind?"

John laughed. "I'll be glad to, but you need to know in advance, this is not my forte. I've been known to cut off heads." He simulated a slashing gesture across his throat. "It's my Sleepy Hollow special."

Jenny giggled. "I'll take my chances, Ichabod."

John walked up the steps to get as much of the fountain in the picture as he could. After clicking a couple of times, he raised his hand and shouted, "I got it."

The lights of Trevi seemed brighter than he remembered them, and the people seemed more animated than before. He wondered why. As he viewed the scene from a distance, John watched his three new friends. Soon his eyes centered on Elaine. He allowed his focus to remain on her for a time, intrigued by what he saw and knowing she was unaware he was watching. He imagined Elaine was in her late forties or early fifties. Her short blond hair fell in soft curls around her face, and she was very pretty. For the first time since Claire's death, he found himself looking at a woman and thinking how lovely she was. Suddenly, noticing such things made him uncomfortable. But he quickly dismissed it. After all this was Rome.

TWELVE

Ponte Vecchio

Jenny noticed the wedding ring on John's finger, and her sighting was no accident. Midway through his Keats talk, her curiosity got the best of her, and a quick glance confirmed her assumption. Meeting someone like him in such a romantic clime, unattached, was to expect the impossible. Later he had alluded to his wife being with him on an earlier trip.

Lying in bed that night she wondered. *Where's his wife now? Why isn't she with him?* Thoughts of that evening's dinner and how she had struggled to keep her eyes off of him replayed in Jenny's mind. She had mostly been successful, limiting her glances to when he was talking, but not always. *I hope no one noticed.*

JENNY KISSED ME!

It was on one of those occasions her earlier sensation of familiarity grew clearer. John had removed his glasses, and she saw his eyes. There was no mistaking who he reminded her of. It was Jonathan. A short time later, for a fleeting moment she even imagined there was a gesture reminiscent of the boy she had loved, though she couldn't be sure. Time had dimmed some memories. As they had made their way to the bus, Kay whispered in Jenny's ear, "I think I'll ask him to join us tomorrow. What do you think?"

Jenny had limited her affirmative response to a nod, not wanting to reveal the powerful emotions building within.

She plumped the pillow, then turned it over. The cool underside felt good to her, since the room was too warm. Jenny inhaled deeply and then blew her breath into the air. She tried to imagine how that Texas boy of forty years ago could have grown into a man very much like this Arizona college professor. She smiled her biggest smile since her plane had landed. *This will be like touring Italy with Jonathan.* After mulling over the thought a few seconds, she suddenly sat up in bed. Shaking her head vigorously, she exclaimed loudly, "It can't be him. It's not possible!" She laid her head back on the pillow. *One in a million.. no way. It's got to be the poetry thing.* Her emotions subsided with the explanation.

Determined to empty her mind of his image so she could get some sleep, she sought a new focus. It was above her. As her eyes scanned the Italian molding on the ceiling, its ornate beauty suggested a preview of what awaited her tomorrow—Florence. In a matter of minutes, she fell asleep.

Jenny awoke an hour before the alarm. Florence lingered in her consciousness. The tour was scheduled to spend the afternoon and the next two nights there. She looked forward to it as much as Rome, and her heart thumped with anticipation. An art appreciation course at UT—reading about the city's galleries and seeing photos of their collections—had created an appetite for Renaissance art, which she had occasionally nourished through the years. Now she would see the actual creations touched by the very fingers of Raphael, Botticelli, daVinci, and Michelangelo. *I'll get to see all of them. I can't believe it.* She knew that the highlight of the day would be Michelangelo's *The David*, the most famous sculpture in the world. Jenny closed her eyes and waited for the alarm to go off. She sighed as her mind made a connection. *We'll celebrate the New Year in Florence, where the Renaissance began—a new millennium in the city of rebirth. I'm so glad I came.*

৵৵৵

At breakfast Kay suggested that the four of them sit on the long back seat of the bus. The time flew by as they talked and laughed. Driving time between Rome and Florence was ordinarily less than three hours, but a planned stop at Pisa en route meant arrival time would not be until early in the afternoon.

The morning was crisp and sunny, perfect for driving through the countryside, which was fresh and clean after a morning shower—a nice change from the gray shades of the city. As the bus came closer to Pisa they saw the famous Leaning Tower in the distance, and John directed a good natured poke at his new friend.

"Bud, see what happens when you turn the world over to building contractors? That's an architectural disaster—and it's theologically flawed, to boot." He tapped Bud's shoulder. "Didn't the founder of Christianity say something about a wise man building on a rock foundation?"

Bud had a quick rejoinder. "That architectural disaster, as you call it, was built over 600 years ago." He returned the tap on John's shoulder. "It's still standing, while your man Keats is horizontal in Rome."

After John chuckled, he said, "Speaking of a wise man, I guess it's foolish to mess with you, huh." He nudged Bud with his elbow. "But I'll probably give it another shot."

After a brief tour of the Leaning Tower and its environs, the four tourists returned to their bus. Since they would arrive in Florence in about an hour, they all put their heads together and planned their free time before dinner. Florence, unlike Rome, was a compact city, making it convenient to experience the sights on foot. They decided to walk to the Arno River and visit the famous medieval bridge, Ponte Vecchio. Then they intended to top off the day by a visit to the Academy of Fine Arts to see the statue of the biblical *David*.

When they arrived at the bridge, the foursome split up to pursue their individual interests. Except for an open section in the middle, Ponte Vecchio was lined with many small tourist shops. After an hour of independent meandering, all but one reunited. John was missing.

They made a quick search and located him in the open section of the bridge, his gaze fixed far out over the river. Bud started to walk over there when Kay suddenly stopped him. "Wait," she cautioned. "Look at him. He's sad. I bet he's thinking about his wife."

"You're right, he probably is," Bud said.

"What do you mean?" Jenny said.

"When we had dinner together the other evening, he talked about her with tears in his eyes," Kay said. "She died about two years ago. He's still grieving. I'm sure there are places filled with memories of her. This bridge must be one."

They waited for a while before Jenny spoke. "He looks so down. I'd like to go over to him. What do you think, Kay?" she said softly.

The answer, though slow in coming, had a confident ring, "That would be nice, Elaine."

Bud joined in. "Good idea. Go cheer him up."

Jenny walked over and stood silently beside John. She looked out over the river and waited for two or three minutes before she turned toward his face. Even from the side, she saw his eyes were teary.

"John, I'm so sorry. Kay told me about your wife." She paused, wondering if she ought to continue. After a moment she spoke, "Does the bridge bring back memories?"

John nodded slowly. A few minutes later the words came out, scarcely audible. "We stood here together…."

JENNY KISSED ME!

"John, I don't know if this will help, but a few years ago after my mother's death, a dear friend said something I've never forgotten. She said the pain I felt was the result of having been granted the most wonderful blessing humans can experience—to love and to be loved." Jenny reached out and gently touched John's hand as she spoke. "It brought me some peace."

John looked down at her hand.

Jenny wondered if he might want to verbalize his feelings, so she gave him an opening. "John, if I'm prying, and you don't want to talk about it, please tell me. But if you'd like to share what happened, I'd love to hear about it."

The tension in John's throat kept him from answering, but the impulse to respond in another way overpowered him, and so for the first time since she had joined him on the bridge he turned and looked at her. Elaine was near, nearer than she had ever been. She smiled—and his sadness began to melt.

"What was your wife's name?" Jenny asked.

"Claire."

He once again looked out over the river. "She was a poetry lover like me, and I had memorized some lines just for her." He turned and glanced at Jenny, then he smiled ever so slightly. "I can still see her face."

Soon John was sharing memories of his wife with this stranger he had met only the day before. He related all that had taken place on the bridge with Claire when he told her the story of Beatrice and Dante. There were no tears this time. And Jenny loved the telling of it.

"I didn't know about Beatrice, but I knew about Dante because he wrote *The Divine Comedy*," she said.

"Have you read it, Elaine?"

"No, but now I think I want to."

"You might want to settle for *Cliff's Notes*. It's a long read, over fourteen thousand lines, but still one of the major works of world literature. It also features Beatrice."

"Really, I wish I knew more about it." Jenny looked at John and teased, "Could you save me a few dollars, and give me 'John's Notes'?"

He laughed, appreciating her repartee. "Well, I'll give it a try. *The Divine Comedy* is a Christian vision of the afterlife. An allegory. Dante goes through three realms of the dead: Inferno, Purgatory, and finally Paradise. That's where Beatrice comes in. She's the ideal woman. She guides him to the Beatific Vision."

"What's that?" Jenny asked.

"Basically, it relates to our perception of God. While on earth, we have an indirect knowledge that relies on prayer and meditation. But in Paradise, it will be different. Beatrice leads Dante to this vision of God. Dante believed experiencing human love could guide one ultimately to God."

At that moment, Bud and Kay walked up. "It's getting late, guys," Bud said. "Before chow time I think we'd better go see that fella who felled the giant."

୬୬୬

Back in her room that evening, Jenny changed into her nightgown. She was thrilled with expectations for tomorrow—New Year's Eve. *We're going to celebrate a new millennium—nothing like it in the last thousand years—and only two days ago, I felt... then I met John.*

JENNY KISSED ME!

Jenny thought about something that occurred earlier that day when the four of them viewed *The David*. While they gazed up at the seventeen-foot marble masterpiece, the guide referred to it as a miracle, detailing how the twenty-six year old Michelangelo had created the work from a block of stone so marred that other sculptors such as Leonardo daVinci had rejected it. When the guide finished, John leaned over and whispered, "Quite a transformation." Jenny looked into his eyes and nodded agreement. If John had been able to read her thoughts, he would have known her gesture didn't refer to the statue, but to the change within her produced at Ponte Vecchio. First the news of John's loss had touched her deeply as she saw his grief. Moments later, while waiting for his response to her question about memories of his wife and Ponte Vecchio, the import of Kay's revelation had struck her—John was single.

In the quietness of her room, as Jenny reviewed the days' events she smiled. Feelings that had been absent for years, feelings she didn't think she was capable of having anymore, feelings that now came only with memories—memories of Jonathan—were slowly coming back again.

৵৵৵

Ponte Vecchio had initially been a setback for John. It was his suggestion that they all separate, having done so for personal reasons. He wanted to be alone on the bridge with his memories of Claire and their kiss. He wanted to experience that moment again. Instead he found only the pain of her absence—until Elaine walked up and silently entered into his emotions.

Her words made a deep impression on him. They had been perfect. He now realized how blessed he was to have known such a love as Claire's. From now on he intended to find happiness in her memory and leave behind the pain of her loss.

But Elaine's appearance brought more than just a new perspective on Claire's death. Something she did, not said, dispelled the hurt—it was her smile. Its tranquilizing effect was immediate, bringing with it a strange sensation of having been there before. Now in his hotel room, the identity of that moment from the past was clear and unmistakable. Forty years ago when he was also in the throes of despondency, he saw a girl smile. Two places—a cafeteria in Texas and a bridge in Italy—so far apart in distance and long separated in years, yet unified by the same feeling.

If you had asked John what memory from the past had been stirred by Elaine's smile on the Ponte Vecchio, all space and time would have vanished and the face of Jenny would have appeared.

THIRTEEN

The Millennium

John set his alarm an hour earlier than normal and arose at five o'clock. It would be around 10 p.m. in the States, and he wanted to call his children to wish them an early Happy New Year. He felt it might be difficult to get through later.

There had been a time when the holiday season, with its opportunities for the family to gather, was John's favorite time of the year. It meant togetherness, laughter, and good times. After Claire died, the Merry vanished from Christmas and the Happy from New Year. Five weeks after her passing, Harper suggested they gather at her home for Christmas, hoping a change in venue might be easier on the family. It hadn't been for John, and it was no different the following year. Now the family occasions Claire had loved so much only magnified her absence. It gave him some relief knowing that this trip would take him away from home much of the holiday season. Nevertheless, as the New Year approached his thoughts again began to drift homeward.

He called Harper first.

"Hello, Sugar, I wanted to wish you an early Happy New Year, while I could get through."

"Happy New Year to you, Pop…or as Sophia Loren would say, *Felice Anno Nuovo*."

"I'm impressed Harp, but I haven't run into her yet…believe me, I'd know it. Now, since you've probably exhausted your Italian vocabulary, what do you guys have planned for tomorrow evening?"

"We're doing something different this year." Harper proceeded with a detailed account of her family's New Year's Eve plans, and then turned her attention to her father.

"Pop, I forgot to ask you before you left, does your tour group have anything special planned for the Millennium celebration?"

"They have a large room reserved at our hotel. Whether any special activities are in the works, I don't know. I'll have to wait and see."

"Well, Pop, are you enjoying yourself?"

"I am. I really am."

"I knew you would. No problems, huh?"

"Well," John hesitated, "there was a rough moment yesterday afternoon at a place your mom and I shared, but it didn't last long. One of the tour members noticed, and had some very thoughtful words to say. The day was really enjoyable after that. Sometime Harper, you

JENNY KISSED ME!

have to make this trip. Just talking about it can't do it justice. You've got to be here."

"Listen, Pop, you don't have to lobby me. If you'll provide the babysitting, Jerry and I will be over there in a New York minute."

"Give those grandkids of mine a couple of more years, and I'll take you up on it."

"Pop, who came to your aid? You've mentioned a couple from Indiana, was it one of them?"

"No, they were there, but it wasn't them. It was a schoolteacher; I think she is from a suburb of Dallas."

"Did you say 'she'?"

"Yes, a lady in our tour group."

"Is she married?" Before her father could respond the next question came. "How old is she?"

"I don't know, Harper," John snapped. "Why are you asking me that?" The silence on the other end allowed him to regain his composure and resume his normal tone with his daughter. "I'd guess she's in her late forties. Just an acquaintance...on the same tour. She came over on the plane with the Indiana couple. They've become friends, so I guess you could say when I started hanging out with them, I inherited her. She was part of the package."

Later when John hung up the phone, he was disappointed in his sharp response to Harper's probing. But, he was not ready to talk to anyone, much less his own daughter, about his attraction to Elaine.

ംംംം

The gang of four gathered at the usual time for breakfast. Excitement was in the air as they made plans for the day.

Kay was the first to speak. "Where are we going, guys? There's a lot to see in Florence."

"Well, art is a must, with all the galleries and museums," John said. He turned to Elaine and added, "You mentioned taking a class in art appreciation. Is there any place special you want to see?"

"I'd like to visit the Uffizi Gallery. It's one of the most famous art museums in the world. They have paintings from all the great artists—Raphael, daVinci, Michelangelo—"

"The trinity of the high renaissance." Kay interrupted.

Her husband looked at the ceiling. "Yeah, that's just what I was going to say."

"Plus, I think Giotto," John added. "They have a painting of his at Uffizi. He's lesser known, but actually started early renaissance art here in Florence two hundred years before those other guys."

"Giotto did more than that," Bud said. "He made quite a contribution to architecture. While the tour group is together, the bus will make its first stop overlooking the city. The most dominate building we'll see is the Florentine Cathedral, and Giotto designed its bell tower."

"Yes, the Cathedral is impressive," John said. "I saw it when Claire and I were here. I think it took almost two hundred years to build, and that octagonal dome is the largest brick dome in the world."

"Yeah, how about four million bricks." Bud said.

JENNY KISSED ME!

John glanced at him and pretended to be serious. "Was that an Acme contract?"

"No, they were tied up with Wile E. Coyote."

"Let's get moving guys." Jenny rose from her chair. "We've got a fun day ahead."

ঙ~ঙ~ঙ

The sun was near to the ground as they walked down the narrow street to their hotel. Jenny's words had been prophetic; it had been a fun day. Though it was impossible to see all the art, they did view a good sampling of famous paintings, and sculptures. Midway through the afternoon as they were leaving an art gallery, Jenny was in high spirits. *It would be a ball going anywhere with this group. Seeing a city like Florence is just icing on the cake.* Her eyes were on John as the thought occurred.

The foursome parted company in the lobby and returned to their rooms for some rest before the evening's activities. As Kay and Bud walked down the hallway, an unseen figure joined them. Before Cupid was through, an elaborate plot was devised to bring two members of the group together for the evening.

"Bud, don't you think Elaine and John like each other?"

"Yes, I also like Elaine and John."

"I mean, don't you believe they make a nice couple?"

"I know what you mean, Dearie. I got the drift of this conversation, before you even completed the sentence."

191

"Hear me out, Honey."

"Don't I always?"

"Bud, ever since they met, you and I have always been along. We've got to get the two of them alone this evening."

"What's this *we* business? You go right ahead, as if it would do any good to suggest otherwise—like allowing nature to take its own course, if nature chooses to do so. So good luck in your, and I emphasize *your*, plot."

"Thanks, for your permission." Kay smiled gleefully. "I've got to get busy, so I'm going down to the lobby for a few minutes."

Forty minutes later, Kay returned to reveal her strategy. "This will be a long evening, from the dinner party all the way into the New Year. If we can arrange for them to be alone for that time, good things will happen."

"If the waiter doesn't trip and dump a bowl of soup in one of their laps."

Kay ignored Bud's statement. "Here's the plan. I'll call Elaine and suggest we drop by her room on our way down to dinner, so she can go with us. I think she'll just take that as a nice gesture on our part—being thoughtful to a woman alone."

"While all the time, 'being thoughtful' has nothing to do with it. It's not thoughtful, it's downright deceptive."

"Maybe it is a little deceptive. But it's thoughtful. I do like her and John, and you know they both like—"

"I know where all of this is going. You believe, Miss Matchmaker, that they ought to like each other so much they end up saying *I do*."

Kay smiled. "You're catching on. But you're ahead of me, honey."

"I am not. I'm just cutting to the chase. Oh well, let's hear it, what's my role in this? Is it major, or am I a supporting actor?"

"Definitely major. Without it, the plan never gets off the ground. When it's time to drop by Elaine's room, I'll show up late and you won't be with me."

"Good, I'll be down in the lounge."

Kay laughed. "No, you won't. Ten minutes before time to go down to dinner, you'll call John and ask him if you can come by his room and borrow a tie."

"Borrow a tie!" Bud threw up his hands. "You have to be kidding. When is the last time you saw me in a tie? Let me rephrase that. When was the last time I went to a funeral?"

"I don't know, but shame on you. It's time you broke the drought."

"What makes you think John has a tie? Why don't I ask him if I could borrow some underwear? I'm sure he has some, though I can't speak from personal experience."

Unwavering, Kay said, "The very first evening John came to dinner, I remember he wore a tie. I noticed it, because he was the only man who was, and I appreciated it."

"But, Dearie, he learned a lesson that evening—you don't wear a tie on your vacation, even if you do wear them to funerals. If you've noticed, that evening was the last time he wore a tie. This is where your scheme falls flat. Wait, let me rephrase that. This is the *first* defect. I predict there'll be more."

"Okay, let's hear it. What's defective?"

"Don't you think it will be a bit suspicious if I, being a slovenly sort of guy, suddenly show up looking like Cary Grant?"

She looked him up and down. "I'll assure you, Bud, no one will make that mistake. You're more the Ernie Borgnine type." She giggled. "Sorry, I couldn't resist. Meanwhile, your digressions are wasting valuable time. We've only got a few more minutes."

"Well, let's get on with it," Bud said with a shrug of resignation.

"I'll go down to dinner with Elaine, and you'll walk down with John. I've already discussed this with our tour guide. She has some cupid in her too and thinks it's a wonderful idea. Why do you think I was gone for forty minutes?"

"You mean you came up with the actual plan in less time? Amazing."

Kay continued undeterred, "In the dining room, each table has four chairs. But Carlita will remove two chairs from one of the tables, so only two people can sit there."

Bud chuckled. "That table is for the victims."

"Exactly. Now both of us will enter late with our unsuspecting friends. We'll leave nothing to chance."

"And you know how we're going to do this, right?"

"I haven't figured out how you're going to arrange it. But if you can design a house, you can certainly manage this. However you do it, *Ernie,* you will need to

194

stall. I will enter the room with Elaine, eight minutes late, while you enter with John, ten minutes late. Got it?"

"Yeah, but that will require us to synchronize our watches, like in those heist movies—you know, where one thief enters the side entrance exactly two and a half minutes after the other thief enters the main entrance."

"Yes, precisely like in the movies. And I've talked with that sweet couple from Albuquerque, the Georges. They're in on this too."

"Who isn't?"

"When I enter with Elaine, Amy George will motion for me to come over to their table. Then, if you don't botch it, you should be entering the room with John. Amy, on cue, will say to me, 'Kay I need to talk to you, would you and Bud join us for dinner?' I'll graciously accept, and then motion for you to join us. Now there is one table left—a table for two. There are two people left standing, Elaine and John. Even you can do the math on this one."

"You want to know the proverbial fly in this ointment? Let's say the plot plays out flawlessly. Nevertheless, Dearie, don't you think when John and Elaine see themselves standing alone in the middle of the room—looking as conspicuous as a fellow wearing a black tuxedo and a pair of brown loafers—they are going to know something's afoot? Kay, it has 'setup' written all over it."

"Hmmm, maybe," Kay admitted.

"Yeah, like the sun rising."

"But what can they do? Which of them is going to hesitate to sit with the other? They're too considerate for that. Once they do sit down together, you watch what happens. They already care for each other. You can see it in their faces. One day soon, they'll thank us for this."

"No, they'll thank you. I want no credit if this succeeds and no blame if it implodes." Bud winked at Kay.

As he got up from his chair and walked toward the closet, Bud suddenly stopped, turned, and looked at Kay with a frown on his face.

"What's the matter?" Kay asked.

The tone of Bud's voice took on a somber note. "What happens if the battery in my watch dies?"

"We'll take our chances, Honey."

ৡৡৡ

Kay's scheme went off with impeccable precision. Jenny and John looked at one another, and then at the empty table.

"Well, will you join me?" John asked as he assisted Jenny with her chair.

Sensing the heat building in her face, Jenny knew what color it was turning. She covered her face with her hand and said, "I'm really embarrassed, John. I didn't have anything to do with this. Believe me."

"Are you sure?" he stretched the last word for emphasis. Then he reached over, touched her hand and said with a chuckle, "We both know who the culprits are." As he spoke, John glanced over at Bud, who had already unencumbered himself of the borrowed necktie.

Bud returned John's glance with a look of unconvincing innocence.

"Elaine, let's play along with them," John said through a Cheshire Cat smile. "We'll exact our retribution later."

"I'm for that—on both counts."

The two of them sat in silence for a few minutes, and then John spoke. "Elaine, I did want to talk with you. Yesterday on the bridge, when I was at such a low, you came to my aid. It was very thoughtful of you."

"I'm glad it helped. I was uneasy about it. It's why I didn't say anything for a few minutes…I wasn't sure what to say."

"What you said was perfect. When I got back to my room, it reminded me of something."

"Anything you'd like to share?"

"I thought about something from the movie *Shadowlands*. Have you seen it?"

"No, I just know it's about C. S. Lewis and the death of his wife."

"What you said on the bridge reminded me of a scene in the movie, where his wife Joy is attempting to prepare Lewis for her impending death. She tells him something like, 'the pain that comes is part of the happiness now….'"

Jenny pondered his thought. "That is insightful. I need to see the movie."

"I need to see it again. It was a favorite of ours. After I lost Claire, I threw it away. Now, I'm ready." He smiled and touched Elaine's hand. "You've helped me."

"Have I?"

"Yes, even before Ponte Vecchio. You and that meddlesome couple over there were responsible for lifting my spirits. Before our group formed, I was pretty miserable—even had some regrets about making this trip."

"Regrets! About what?" Bud's big frame hovered over them.

John shot back, "About loaning you my favorite tie. You were sailing under false colors, my friend. By the way, where is it?"

Bud shook his head. "I'm not sure. I think I accidently flushed it down the toilet."

"Well, go find a plumber. You wanted us to be alone. You got your wish, so now beat it." John winked at Elaine.

The conversation ceased momentarily as the waiter served their first course. After a few minutes, Jenny asked about John's children and grandchildren, an interest John was more than happy to enlighten. When he finished telling Jenny about all of them, she said, "It sounds like you have been blessed with a lovely family. I know you're proud of all of them."

John nodded and then turned his attention to Jenny.

"What about your family?" John said.

Jenny's face grew somber. "There's nothing much to say. I've been married twice and both were disappointments."

"Do you have children?"

"No, we never had any. It wasn't due to any lack of desire on my part. I always wanted some." Her shoulders seemed to slump with resignation as she shook her head. "It just never worked out." Elaine lowered her gaze, as she locked an unfocused stare on the table.

There was silence.

"I'm sorry Elaine."

She lifted her head up and revealed a slight smile. "There's been some compensation. I've taught elementary students for over thirty years now, so I've had quite a few kids."

"You don't look old enough to have taught that long." Unable to hide the surprise in his voice, he added, "You really don't."

"Well, I'm fifty-seven."

"My, the years have been good to you. You're the same age as I am. When did you graduate from high school?"

"1960."

He reached across and put his hand up. "Give me five, Elaine. We're classmates!"

When the final course for dinner was served, the evening turned into dancing for some of the group. John and Jenny continued to talk, gradually moving to happy topics, friendly teasing, and laughter.

As the evening progressed and Kay noticed the two frequently laughing and totally focused on each other, she nudged Bud, rolled her eyes and smiled. Bud just tilted his head and shrugged with a reluctant grin.

Shortly before midnight, John, Jenny, Kay, and Bud gathered with other tour members to sample a festive buffet table bountifully covered with fresh snacks, pastries, and finger foods. While they were talking, Jenny whispered in Kay's ear so softly no one else could hear, "Thank you." Kay smiled at her, and then widened it as she looked over at her husband who watched with interest.

They were all still talking at the buffet when the traditional countdown began. As soon as the clock hands pointed to midnight, everyone filled the room with shouts of "Happy New Year!" That was a spontaneous cue for all to join in *Auld Lang Syne*. When the song ended, John and Jenny were forced to go in different directions as they mingled with the group and continued the festivity. As the noise started to die down, they gradually started sifting their way through the crowd and met back at their table.

"Just like home," Jenny said as she sat down, "even singing *Auld Lang Syne*. That was a surprise."

"Well, it's hardly an American song. English speaking people around the world sing it."

"Really? I didn't know that. I'm embarrassed to say I don't even know what the words mean, and I'm a teacher." She laughed.

"Well, I'm familiar with it, because it pertains to poetry."

"I can believe that. I'd like to hear about it."

"It's actually a Scottish poem. The words convey the idea of days gone by, or long ago."

"Who wrote the poem?"

"A very famous romantic poet, Robert Burns."

Jenny's stare passed right through John as a long ago scene in the library flashed briefly in her mind. She giggled softly. "Are you sure it wasn't George?"

He looked back at her, puzzled by the moment's familiarity.

JENNY KISSED ME!

Jenny broke the spell by rising from her chair. She walked around the table, leaned over, and kissed John on the cheek.

"Happy New Year!"

FOURTEEN

A MEMORY REVISITED

The kiss had an effect on both John and Jenny. Though they remained at the table for what seemed like hours (only a few minutes), the mood strangely altered. Conversation ceased. Uncomfortable with the silence, John struggled to find appropriate words. "Jenny, I think we… I mean, we…it's really getting late."

"Yes, it is late. I can walk back to my room with Bud and Kay. See you in the morning, John."

"It already is morning, Elaine," he said with a half-hearted chuckle that felt all wrong. So he turned away with a casual wave of his hand.

ی‌ی‌ی

JENNY KISSED ME!

Though John and Jenny parted company, neither could part with the emotions the kiss had wrought. Those went with them to their rooms, along with thoughts of days gone by—memories of a boy, a girl, and a kiss.

When John opened the door to his room, he glanced at his watch. The time was almost one o'clock. Without removing his clothes, he fell onto the bed, flat on his back, hands clasped behind his head, eyes focused on the ceiling. The already abbreviated night would be shortened still. He had known it the moment Elaine kissed him.

What had occurred had been so familiar. The parallel baffled him. It was like the library scene forty years ago. He had replayed it so many times that he could even recall the conversation leading up to the kiss. *I'd even jokingly said something about George Burns.* He slowly shook his head. The names were different, the times and places were different, but the story line was eerily the same—the chair, the kiss, even the feeling that followed. The poem "Jenny Kissed Me" had happened again. Though he marveled at the mystery of it all, he could not welcome the powerful emotions produced in its aftermath.

Determined to rid himself of those feelings, he got up and walked over to the closet. He looked down and smiled. There in the luggage was a remedy—the volume of poetry from his *Harvard Classics* series. It contained the poem "Jenny Kissed Me". He paused before opening the suitcase, recalling how despondent he had been at the time of the poem's discovery that summer prior to his senior year. Once again he would use its powers to alter his emotions by reminding him of the girl in its title. Thoughts of her could drive these uninvited feelings about Elaine from his mind. He was comfortable with feelings about someone in the past, as he had experienced on the flight over—Jenny was only a remembrance, she was never a threat to Claire. Elaine was different. She was a present reality and he could never allow her access into his heart. That was reserved for Claire and always would be. He reaffirmed his credo. *Romantics are forever people.*

Retrieving the book, he sat down in a chair. After slowly reading each line of the poem, his thoughts first drifted to the prominent place it had occupied through his high school years and finally to how it had resurfaced unexpectedly on two occasions in the years that followed...

It was the spring semester of his third year teaching at the university, and he was in the classroom lecturing on Romantic poetry. He had just cited Wordsworth's famous work, *Lyrical Ballads*, and shared a quote from it. "Poetry is the spontaneous overflow of powerful emotions." To further emphasize the concept, he recited the closing lines of Shelly's classic "Love's Philosophy."

> "See! the mountains kiss high heaven,
> And the waves clasp one another;
> No sister flower would be forgiven
> If it disdained its brother;
> And the sunlight clasp the earth,
> And the moonbeams kissed the sea:

JENNY KISSED ME!

> What are all these kissings worth
> If thou kiss not me?"

A hand shot up. "That poem reminds me of one written by Leigh Hunt. Is he one of the major romantic poets?"

John responded, "Hunt never attained the status of the Big Six, as they were called—Blake, Coleridge, Byron, Keats, Shelly and Wordsworth. However, he was a significant impetus to the Romantic Movement. It's apropos you'd mention his name following a poem by Shelly. Were you aware they were close friends?"

"No, I wasn't."

"There is a well-known painting of Shelly's funeral. He drowned during a storm while sailing off the coast of Italy, and his body was cremated right on the shore. The painting features three men on the beach around the funeral pyre. One is Byron, another is Leigh Hunt. Which of Hunt's poems were you thinking of?"

The student laughed. "Well, all that 'kissing' reminded me of the poem, 'Jenny Kissed Me.'"

John's eyes turned from the young man toward the class, as the words flowed spontaneously,

> "Jenny kissed me when we met,
> Jumping from the chair she sat in...."

Midway through it, he noticed all faces were riveted on him. As he closed out the poem, his eyes scanned the room. An uneasy self-consciousness swept over him. He looked at his watch and found deliverance.

"I guess you can leave early today, but remember, you owe me five."

Some laughed. None complained.

John hurriedly grabbed his notes and headed to his office. Aware someone was behind him, he turned to see the young man who had asked the question, along with a girl.

She spoke first. "Dr. Kaelin, I love it when you recite poetry, but that last one was the best ever. You seemed to have been really moved by it."

Her words rekindled John's embarrassment, which had begun to wane.

"It's just an old favorite of mine I hadn't thought about in a long time. I was caught off-guard," he said, nodding toward the young man who had asked the question.

"I didn't mean to put you on the spot, Dr. Kaelin. But she's right. I'd read that poem a number of times, but you made it come alive."

John had an off period following the class. It was noon and he usually spent the time in his office with a sack lunch Claire had prepared for him. Normally there was a sandwich or chips in one hand while the other turned the pages of an open book.

That day was not normal. The poem had returned and revived feelings he thought had been left behind. For the first time since he and Claire were married he visualized the girl in the poem. As he allowed pictures of Jenny to pass before him: in the cafeteria, in the library, on prom night, and finally, that last night at graduation, he was curious what had happened to her. *She's probably married and has a family. I wonder if she ever went back to San Marcos*. He put his sandwich down on the desk and picked up the framed picture of Claire that sat nearby, turning his thoughts back to her. By the time he returned the photo to his desk, thoughts of the girl and the poem were forgotten once again—immersed in his subconscious for another quarter of a century until the conversation six days ago with a stranger on the plane brought them back to life…

John glanced at the clock on his hotel room's bedside table. It was 3:30 and he was suddenly spent. The book was still in his lap, opened to the poem. He tapped the page with his fingers. "You just won't go away," he muttered.

ಆಆಆ

The conversation was minimal as a preoccupied Jenny joined Kay and Bud for the walk back to her room. She was deep in thought as she pondered the evening's final event. *I wonder if Bud and Kay saw me kiss him.* Then curiosity turned to grave concern. *What did John think about the kiss? I acted as if I was totally oblivious to the fact that he's still in love with his wife. He couldn't dismiss it as nothing more than a New Year's Eve kiss. It happened too late in the evening for that. And his reaction afterwards…he was clearly uncomfortable.* She shook her head. *Oh, why did I do that?*

As she reached her room, she was finally able to halt the relentless replay of the event by telling herself what happened, had happened, and could not be undone. Still the thought gnawed at her. *How can I face him in the morning?*

Some thirty minutes later just as she was drifting off to sleep, the scene flashed before her a final time. But on this occasion the face across the table changed. It was no longer John, but a boy sitting in the school library, and she was kissing him on the very spot she had kissed John that evening. It startled her awake. Now she knew why she had acted so impulsively.

An unfathomable calm enveloped her as the scene from her past gave her a very different perspective on what had happened…

Forty years ago, although the feelings following the kiss were the same, she had kept them secret. She remembered the probing of a friend that day in the library, when she returned to the table.

"Jenny, what was that all about?"

She shrugged her shoulders. "Jonathan's a good friend. That's all,"

All eyes were on her as another friend chided, "You have a bunch of good friends. But you don't usually kiss them in the library."

"We came here to study, so let's do it." Jenny raised her voice. "It was nothing." The moment she said the words she knew that was not the case, and that evening confirmed it.

'Nothing' does not prevent sleep, as the unrelenting striking of the clock signals the passing of the hours.

'Nothing' does not keep reoccurring to you for days thereafter.

JENNY KISSED ME!

'Nothing' only becomes nothing when you allow it to die...

Jenny had done that once. Then, like Lazarus, it came back to life at the opening of a shoebox. The secret beneath the lid was that a capricious kiss in the library may have been the most honest expression of her feelings in all those school years. She had revealed the true longings of her heart.

Now, her perspective did a turnabout and she was thrilled that the evening's kiss had happened. *A second chance. This time I won't hide my heart.* For a final time, she replayed the kiss on John's cheek, only this time unaccompanied by regret. As her eyelids gently closed, an explosion of warmth spread throughout her body. The evening's trauma had turned to triumph.

❦❦❦

Kay and Bud managed scant more sleep than Jenny and John. Following the New Year's celebration, Kay returned to their room ecstatic and eager to talk about how beautifully her plan had worked. Bud, the only one present, was a reluctant audience.

"When you saw Elaine whisper in my ear, do you know what she said?"

"She said she was sleepy and wanted to go to bed."

"Bud, the sooner we talk about this the sooner you'll get to bed. So for your own good, keep the interruptions to a minimum."

"Yes Ma'am."

"Did you see what a great time they had together?"

"I did, and if I hadn't had to wear a tie, I would have been having just as good a time as they were."

Kay threw up her hands in disbelief. "What a phony you are. You didn't have a tie on for more than five minutes, so let's not hear any more of that."

Wearily Bud said, "Kay, I surrender. It was a good idea. It worked. They like each other. Now can I get some sleep?"

"Did you see Elaine kiss him?"

"So what. Everybody was kissing. It was New Year's Eve. You even kissed that strange little man from Poughkeepsie. I think you kissed everybody but me."

"There." Kay planted a kiss on Bud lips. "I'm sorry, I was celebrating. Besides, I can kiss you anytime. But now, this is what we must do."

"Oh, no, another plan."

"Yes, tomorrow you and I will sit together on the bus, so John and Elaine can sit together."

"What if Elaine wants to sit with that guy from Poughkeepsie?"

"I'll leave that to you," Kay said with a laugh. "You're bigger than he is."

The conversation went on for another fifteen minutes, but Kay was not sure Bud was awake for the finish.

ം‌ം‌ം

When the sleep-deprived foursome met for breakfast New Year's morning, it was evident the late hours had taken their toll. Within seconds of sitting down, Bud had a proposal. "Let's say we all agree to keep deathly silent until we finish this first cup of joe, and I mean down to the last drop." No one spoke a word or even gave a nod. The pact was sealed by a sound—the clinking of four cups of coffee in the center of the table.

Later as they headed for the bus, a caffeine-revived Kay announced, "Bud, I guess I'm going to have to sit with you this morning. We need to talk about something." Looking first at one and then at the other, Kay asked casually, "You two don't mind sitting together do you?"

After they exchanged quick glances, Jenny warned, "Watch out Kay, this is Italy."

"What in the world is that supposed to mean?" Kay said.

"Italy is the home of Pinocchio, and you know what happened to a certain part of his anatomy when he engaged in deception."

Bud said, "I love it. Look it's already started to grow."

John continued the fun as they boarded the bus. He looked over his shoulder and said, "Kay, Elaine and I will sit together. But, we'll be sure to sit behind you—just in case it doesn't stop."

ഔഔഔ

En route to Venice, they visited Verona. Their first stop was one of the city's major attractions—a Roman amphitheater completed about the time of Christ yet still used for shows, fairs, opera, and other public events. Then they spent time exploring the town, searching for highlights.

About an hour into their roaming, Jenny spotted a large group of tourists.

"I wonder what that crowd is over there."

"That's the locale of the famous balcony scene," Kay said. "You know, 'Romeo, Romeo, where for art thou Romeo?'"

"Really? I want to see that," Jenny said, grabbing her arm.

They all walked toward the balcony, and Bud asked, "What about it Professor. You're a Shakespeare man. Do you think this is where it happened?"

John shrugged. "Millions come here imagining it to be the place." He pointed toward the bronze statue of Juliette. "'When the legend becomes fact print the legend.'"

"I know that one." Bud chuckled. "It's the best quote I've heard from you yet."

"I thought it might be familiar, but I don't imagine the ladies have the slightest idea what we're talking about."

Kay overheard them. "No secrets, guys. You're dying to tell us anyhow."

"John Wayne, *The Man Who Shot Liberty Valance,*" her husband responded. "I think you missed that movie, dear wife. You were busy watching *Pillow Talk.*"

"What does a cowboy movie have to do with Italy?" Kay asked.

"You've heard of spaghetti westerns." Bud arched his eyebrow.

JENNY KISSED ME!

"Oh, Please." Kay rolled her eyes.

Jenny said, "John, I'd like to know about *Romeo and Juliette*. I only know it's a story about ill-fated lovers."

"Have you seen the musical *Westside Story*?"

Jenny and Kay both nodded.

"I'll abstain," Bud mumbled.

"You've seen it. I had to drag you there." Kay tapped his arm with the back of her hand.

"Sans tie, I imagine," John said.

"I should have gone sans brain," Bud said. "The movie begins with two gangs that meet one another in the street to do battle, and they start dancing. Who can buy that?"

"Suspension of belief, Dear…after all, it's a movie." Kay said.

"John, I'm still waiting to hear about *Romeo and Juliette*." Jenny laughed.

"Okay Elaine, *Westside Story* is based on *Romeo and Juliette,* although in Shakespeare's play, they're feuding families, not gangs. Both have star-crossed lovers. In the movie, they're Tony and Maria."

He turned to Bud. "Here's something you'd appreciate. *Romeo and Juliette* also begins with a street brawl between the families." John grinned. "But they don't dance."

An hour later, Jenny and John walked ahead of their companions toward the bus and soon were out of earshot.

Jenny said, "Shakespeare has to be one of the most quotable people who ever lived. Do you have a favorite quote of his?"

213

John hesitated for a moment before his response, "It's probably one of his more famous ones, from *Hamlet*—'This above all: To thine own self be true....'"

As he finished, Bud called his name. John turned to wait for him.

Jenny said, "John, I'm going ahead. I'll see you on board."

The bus was parked several blocks away, and Jenny was grateful for Bud's sudden intervention. She wanted some privacy to think about the words she just heard. They seem to come at the perfect time. 'To thine own self be true....' As she pondered them, they reinforced the resolve she had reached earlier that morning in her room—to be honest about her feelings. She spoke softly under her breath, "This time, I'm not going to hide them."

FIFTEEN

Prom Night Remembered

As the bus made the journey to Venice, the consensus of the two couples was the late hours on New Year's Eve had taken their toll. Consequently they all looked forward to the "City of Water" as a place to find a hotel, a bed, and a good night's sleep. The numerous and famous sights of the city could wait. Since tour members were on their own for dinner that evening, all agreed they would take advantage of room service and retire early. Conversation slowed as some dozed and others looked through the windows at the passing scenery.

Later in the afternoon as water appeared on the horizon, the massive cruise liner docked in the harbor told them Venice was near.

"John," Kay said, "I just realized Venice is another Italian setting for a Shakespeare play."

"And it doesn't end with *The Merchant of Venice*," John said. "A part of *Othello* is also set right here in Venice."

"Did Shakespeare spend time in Italy?" Jenny asked.

"I don't think so, even though some have surmised that he did. Most scholars and biographers believe he never left England. However, Elizabethans of his time were fascinated with Italian literary works and culture, so Shakespeare had ample access to the information he needed to produce his Italians settings."

Realizing he sounded too much like a professor, John glanced over at Bud, who was obviously not interested in The Bard.

"Bud, I have a question more to your liking. It's about a movie whose final scene is set in Venice. Our hero and a blond are in a boat, and he's tossing some film into the water. Can you name the character?"

"That's a gimme. It's James Bond. And how about some extra credit. The movie is *From Russia with Love*."

"Forget the extra stuff; you only get half credit. Your answer's not precise enough."

"Bond ... James Bond."

"You got it. I knew you'd come through."

"Back to Shakespeare, guys," Kay said. "How about a quote from the *Merchant of Venice*?"

John took a moment and replied, "Here's an example of how phrases from Shakespeare become part of the language, yet most people don't know where they came from. Did you ever hear, 'Love is blind…'?"

Kay nodded.

"Well, the rest of the quote is '…and lovers cannot see the pretty folly that themselves commit.'"

The conversation between Kay, Bud, and John continued, but Jenny became unusually silent after she heard John's words.

ର୍ଚ୍ଚର

The day was almost gone when their tour bus arrived at the edge of Venice, and John was glad to reach the hotel. It had been a full day. Although he was tired and expected to fall asleep, his mind did not cooperate. He couldn't help but wonder about Elaine's silence after his Shakespeare quote.

The next morning John awoke refreshed. Before breakfast, he spent his time alone just outside of the hotel, anticipating the day. As he scanned the canal, he took in all the new sights and sounds. Since he had not seen Venice on his earlier trip, he awaited making new memories in the most unique city in the world.

After breakfast, the group visited a number of shops, museums, and cathedrals. Crossing the bridges, they marveled at the distinctive ambiance of the main canal, constantly in motion with water taxis, water buses, and cargo boats.

Late in the afternoon, they boarded a gondola and watched the gondolier, in his stripped shirt and dapper straw hat, maneuver the boat silently along the narrow passages. The sun, low on the horizon, glistened on top of the waves as they moved soundlessly toward the edge of the canals. Experiencing Venice was a whole new world to John, void of any sense that Claire was not there with him. As they glided, John glanced at Jenny and found her looking at him. No words were spoken.

When the gondola finally pulled up to the pier, Kay said, "You guys must have dinner at the Piazza San Marco, the main square in the city. It's an unforgettable Venice experience. Bud and I have done it several times, so we're going to try a new restaurant tonight…just the two of us."

Touching her nose, Jenny glanced over at John and back at Kay. "Remember?"

Kay clasped her husband's hand as they walked away and said, "We gotta go. Have fun kids."

ର୍ଚ୍ଚର୍ଚ୍ଚ

It was well into the evening when John and Jenny entered San Marco. The piazza was packed with people. Pausing at the entrance and taking in the vastness of the area, Jenny whispered to her companion, "I understand why Napoleon referred to this as 'The Drawing Room of Europe.'" With stars above and lights glittering on the surrounding shops and restaurants, the piazza was alive with the activities of people eating, laughing, and talking. The scene was spectacular. Tables from the restaurants overflowed the edges of the open space. They spotted three chamber orchestras on different sides of the square and noticed several couples dancing. John and Jenny's eyes wandered from scene to scene,

JENNY KISSED ME!

enjoying the atmosphere as they walked through the area on the way to a table. John stopped and nodded toward one on the outside edge of the piazza, close to one of the orchestras. Jenny smiled her approval.

In the typical Italian style they had become accustomed to, their waiter dismissed any awareness of time as he served them. While the entire full course dinner was delicious, they both agreed the special truffle sauce on the entrée was out-of-this-world tasty. During the meal there was no lack of conversation and laughter as each dish was served, but later as they listened to the orchestra, John noticed Elaine seemed bothered. He'd observed the same expression on her face earlier on the bus.

"Elaine, at times today, you've seemed absorbed in thought. I don't mean to intrude, but just wondered if I might help. I remember one time at a certain bridge, you came to my rescue."

Jenny glanced down. "It was the Shakespeare quote, the one about love being blind. It brought back some bad memories."

"You're talking about your marriages?"

Jenny nodded.

"Would you like to talk about it?"

"I don't know…I think… I think I would."

"I think you should," John said softly.

She paused. "In my first marriage, I fell for charm and good looks. I was blind to other things."

"You hadn't known him for long?"

"Long enough…about three years."

"But you didn't see the real person?"

"Before we married, I did see. But I still paid a price." Jenny sighed. "By then the wedding had been planned. It involved my parents. So I convinced myself that he would change, and I went through with the marriage."

"I guess that's not unusual when we're in love. I suppose it's part of the blindness. But it's sad when change doesn't happen."

"That wasn't the saddest thing." Jenny paused. "There was another boy, someone I had loved in high school... I might have married him."

"What happened to him?"

"I can't say. I lost track of him...but, that's history now."

John waited awhile before he said, "Tell me about your second husband."

"Well, it wasn't a good marriage either. It was the typical case of reaction to the first failure. Earlier, I fell for the physical attraction thing. The second time, I was determined that would not be the case." She sighed and looked down. "That husband was killed in an accident."

"Oh, I didn't know that."

Judging by her demeanor, John suspected Elaine was hiding something, something she had a need to reveal. He placed his hand over hers and asked softly, "Can you tell me about it?"

At first Jenny hesitated. She had kept silent for so many years. But something about John made her feel safe, something she couldn't quite identify. She slowly told her story.

"I'd been single for six years after my divorce. I was lonely and looking for companionship, for security." She shook her head. "A relationship needs so much more than that." With a painful look, she continued. "I was oblivious to the fact we didn't really share important things. You know… interests, values, priorities…" She paused. "…and dreams."

"You said he died in an accident. Was it a car wreck?"

"Yes, he was drunk. Fortunately, it didn't involve anyone else…."

Her voice faltered, and she gulped a quick breath. "I don't think I felt anything at his funeral. Just relief." A tear glistened on her cheek. "I feel terrible about that." As she continued, she didn't look at John, but spoke with a frozen gaze. "He had an alcohol problem…he treated me so…so…horribly! He would get drunk…and he…and he…" Her head dropped. "Once I went to the hospital—" Words stopped and the tears poured.

John walked to her side of the table. He took both of Jenny's hands and drew her up next to him. He held her tight and stroked her hair as she leaned on his shoulder. Her long-stored tears flowed. Others around them may have noticed. It didn't matter. After the final tears subsided, they stood for several minutes, Jenny's face still buried in John's shoulder.

Finally, her face reappeared, eyes red and cheeks tearstained, yet clothed with serenity and even the glimpse of a smile. "I've never told anyone that. It just came out."

"I know you haven't. I'm glad you did." Then, giving her a quick wink, he said, "That makes us even."

"Thank you for listening." Jenny smiled. "And for the use of your shoulder."

John looked toward the orchestra and said. "Since we're standing, we might as well take advantage of the music." He took her hand and led her to where several couples were dancing.

Jenny followed reluctantly. "I'm not sure you won't regret this. I haven't danced in years. Neither of my husbands did. I don't think I've danced since my high school senior prom."

"It's something you don't forget. Like…oaring a gondola. Well, I guess." He grinned. "Anyway, we can't pass up this music. If you won't step on my toes, I won't kick you in the shins."

Jenny's concern vanished in an instant as the two synchronized with the music. John's firm hand on her back made following second nature. It seemed like dancing together was something they had always done.

A scene from the past entered the present. She was in San Marcos, her partner was Jonathan, and the music was the theme from *A Summer Place*. Jenny smiled. *That was San Marcos, and this is the piazza at San Marco. It's almost the same…It feels the same.*

She started to tell John of the coincidence, but kept silent, since it would mean nothing to him. However, as they danced longer into the night, that memory from years ago did not go away.

The crowd gradually broke up until there were just a few couples left dancing. The evening was about to end, but as they danced to the last song, she realized the scars of the past were finally exorcised. At last, she had been able to trust someone with her pain.

JENNY KISSED ME!

When the band played its last refrain and the music ended, they agreed it was time to find their way back to the hotel. John reached for her hand, and she felt his strong fingers close around hers as they walked.

Leaving the Piazza, they entered a narrow street—more like a sidewalk—just wide enough for two to walk side by side. There were lanterns at intervals along the way, and the sounds from the main canal along with the noise of laughter from a nearby street, created a magical atmosphere, distinctly Venetian. As they strolled the winding streets back to the hotel, Jenny was engulfed by déjà vu. *Just like my prom night so long ago, I won't ever forget this evening.*

As they finally approached the hotel, John said, "Elaine, do you realize you have a very romantic name?"

"Are you talking about Elaine and Lancelot?"

"Yes, and I was especially thinking of a famous poem by Tennyson, 'The Lady of Shallot'. Are you familiar with it?"

"I've heard of it…that's all."

"Well, the same Lady Elaine was the inspiration for it."

"I didn't know that."

John stopped, and turned to Jenny. "At the end of the poem Lancelot says of Elaine, '… she has a lovely face; God in his mercy lend her grace, The Lady of Shallot.'"

He smiled and looked into Jenny's eyes. "I think Lancelot was right."

ه‍ه‍ه‍

At the window in his room, John looked out over the canal lights. He knew sleep would be minimal, just as it was the night after the kiss. But he didn't care, he didn't even try. He couldn't—wouldn't—leave this wonderful feeling behind so quickly.

He had experienced it twice before—as a boy when he first saw Jenny, and as a young man when he kissed Claire on the dormitory steps.

John tried to picture Claire in his mind, her image gradually fading. But it didn't hurt as much as he thought it would.

SIXTEEN

Catacombs

*T*he return trip to Rome began early the next morning, and the travelers arrived shortly before one o'clock. Tour members were at liberty for the remainder of the day. Before leaving the states, John had carefully planned the final hours of his last full day in Italy. The highlight of the day would be seeing the catacombs. He and Claire had missed them on their previous trip.

As the others went to check out their rooms, John picked up his room key and slipped away to the site of San Calisto, the oldest Christian cemetery in Rome. It was located on the Appian Way, the most important of all the ancient Roman roadways, portions of which dated back to the fourth century B.C.

He arrived at San Calisto ahead of schedule and waited for the tour to begin. As he perused the brochure on the catacombs, a familiar voice spoke his name.

Eyes widening, he looked up and saw Elaine.

She smiled. "I think I caught you trying to sneak away from me."

Taken by surprise, John didn't know what to say. He managed a clumsy, "I didn't think you'd be interested."

Before Jenny could respond, the guide called for the tour to begin, and they followed a group of about thirty people into the catacombs. Their conversation was interrupted for the next forty minutes as they looked and listened.

When it was over Jenny was the first to speak. "John, I noticed the look on your face when we were in the Cubicle of the Sacraments. I can tell you're a Christian."

John nodded. "And a church history buff. It's another reason I'm so fascinated with this city. Rome plays quite a role in the early years of Christianity."

"Maybe you can explain something to me."

"I'll try."

"I always thought Christians gathered in these catacombs to escape persecution. But the guide said they met to unite with other Christians buried there."

"According to what I've read, the guide was correct, although your impression is a popular one."

"Really. Fill me in."

"The frescos of baptism and the Eucharist on the wall in the Cubicle were symbols, which linked those

JENNY KISSED ME!

Christians to departed believers. When they took communion, they believed it united them not only to one another, but to their spiritual ancestors—many martyred for their faith."

John glanced at Elaine. "I had planned to go for a walk on the Appian Way. Would you like to go?"

"Yes, I've looked forward to it." She glanced at the sky. "And the weather's perfect today."

As they strolled, John reached out unconsciously, taking Jenny's hand. "Do you know who walked this road almost two thousand years ago?"

"The Apostle Paul. And I believe he was later beheaded here in Rome during Nero's reign." Jenny winked. "Is that right?"

John winked back.

"John, have you always been a believer?"

"I was raised in the tradition, but later spent a few years in agnosticism."

"Really, tell me about it."

"I grew up going to church, but my faith was shallow. I found that out when I ran into my first atheist."

"Was that in high school?"

"No, I think finding an atheist in high school then was as rare as finding a communist."

Jenny squeezed his hand. "You can spare me the commentary. Please go on."

"It happened my first year of college. I started running around with a guy who told me he was an atheist while we were drinking beer one day. I laughed, assuming he was joking. He was not. Even though he was a bit tipsy, he was pretty convincing."

"What did he say?"

"He didn't phrase it like this at the time, but what he had to say was based on some psychological and anthropological theories about the origin of religion. The views associated with names like Feuerbach, Freud, and Marx. Are you familiar with them?"

"'Religion is the opiate of the people.'"

"Yes, that was Karl Marx's famous slogan. Personally, I doubt whether my buddy was familiar with any of those names. He was hardly an intellectual. As far as Marx goes, he would not have known Karl from Groucho or Harpo. He was just parroting some ideas that made for good beer talk."

Jenny shook her head, "I haven't heard of Feuerbach."

"Neither had he." Then John grinned, "Anheiser and Busch probably exhausted his knowledge of German philosophers."

Then John adopted a more serious tone, "Feuerbach is not as well-known as the others, but he came first and had quite an influence on Marx. He was a philosopher and anthropologist who posited religion as mere wish fulfillment. The gist of his theory was that humans feel trapped in a world full of fears. Feeling helpless, they imagine some idealized being can help them—a God who is benevolent and powerful. The inference is God did not create us; we created him."

"And you believed it?"

"It didn't recruit me to the atheist camp, but the theory was enticing enough for me to abandon my superficial faith. I became an agnostic, and it sure had an impact on my life."

"How?"

"Life was meaningless."

"You became a nihilist?"

"Pretty much so…though I hid it from others. On the outside, I was happy-go-lucky; inside I was miserable. Let's face it; the belief that existence is an accident is pretty depressing stuff."

"What happened to change you?"

"I had begun to work my way out of that philosophy, about the same time as I met Claire."

"Work your way out…. What do you mean?"

"It really began with a quote I heard in a Philosophy course I took my senior year. Francis Bacon said it. Heard of him?"

Jenny nodded. "What did he say?"

"Bacon said something about how a little philosophy will incline your mind to atheism, but depth in philosophy will incline you to religion. I decided my rejection of God had been more than a bit premature, so I determined to change that."

Jenny saw a faint smile on his lips. "What's the matter am I missing something?"

"No, but I did... a bunch of classes that semester. I spent so much time—reading and thinking—while pursuing the topic that my grades took a tumble, but I survived…and it was well worth it."

John paused. "Incidentally, in the process it dawned on me the reason I had rejected theism was because of a psychological argument, and that approach cuts both ways—'what's sauce for the goose is sauce for the gander,' right?"

Jenny nodded, "Go on."

"There are also psychological reasons why one would wish God didn't exist—you get to be your own god, with no ultimate accountability."

John paused, "Pride, the first deadly sin, can be a pretty dominant psychological factor in human behavior, don't you think?"

Jenny's face reflected her agreement. "Please continue,… I'm fascinated."

"In the end, I concluded the case for God—especially ethical monotheism—was compelling, so I began to read the Bible. That's where Claire came in."

"Claire was a believer?"

"Very much so…and she led with her life. Besides—" he winked—"she had pretty eyes. That clinched it."

After they had walked for some time, the couple turned to head back.

"Elaine," John said with a playful grin, "could I interest you in a date? I know a super restaurant. Claire and I ate there when we were here. The food is the best, and I think you'll like the ambiance. What do you say?"

"Hmm, let me think. Yes, I believe I might squeeze you into my schedule," she said, pressing his hand, "but isn't it a little early. After all, this *is* Italy."

"Well, I just wanted to make sure no one beat me to it. After all, a good lookin' woman like you, in Rome."

Jenny beamed. "Could I suggest something to do before dinner?"

"I wish you would."

"Before I left the states, I checked on some things to do during my free time."

"I think I know," John interrupted. "You decided you wanted to spend time with a handsome stranger you'd meet in Rome, right?"

"Yes, but since I haven't found him, I've come up with an alternative."

John laughed heartily, then pretended to flick a tear from his eye and said, "Alright let's hear it."

"I love the sculpture of the Roman fountains. I'd like to see more of them."

"Got any in mind?"

"We might have time for *Four Rivers* and *The Triton*. I've read about Bernini, Michelangelo's successor."

"Great idea, Elaine. We could have kind of a mini *Roman Holiday*."

"I'm ready."

John extended his arm. "Well, let's go Princess."

SEVENTEEN

CANDLELIGHT

Several hours later, John and Jenny were in a cab driving toward the edge of Rome—at least it looked that way to Jenny, as the trees grew thicker and the buildings fewer. When they arrived at their destination, they left the cab and started walking down a garden pathway. Lights flickered in the distance and music and laughter grew as they came near the entrance. The walkway widened to expose an extensive, vine-covered pergola decorated with tiny white lights, hanging over tables covered with red-and-white-checkered cloths and centered with tall silver candelabras.

Jenny squeezed John's arm. "This is beautiful. How did you know I love candlelight?"

They followed the waiter to a secluded table toward the back, placed their orders and resumed talking about the sites they had seen earlier. When the restaurant serenader walked up to their table and began singing "Al di La," Jenny stopped in mid-sentence.

John watched her until the final note of the song. Then he spoke. "Did that bring a special memory?"

"It sure did. Hearing that song is what gave me the idea to make this trip."

"You looked so serious at the end of the song."

"Well, I heard it a few months ago while I was driving home from work. It just occurred to me, I wouldn't be here if that hadn't happened."

"It's strange about those things." Then he smiled broadly. "I'm sure glad you had your radio on."

Their eyes met. Then the words came out.

"Elaine, I was just wondering if you've ever thought of marrying again?" John felt uncomfortable the moment the words passed through his lips.

Jenny took a moment to respond, "I'm not sure. You know, I had a conversation with a friend at the airport before I left. She brought up the subject of romance at this stage in my life. At the time I resisted the idea, pretty emphatically. Now I don't—"

She paused and John jumped into the gap. "I know, Italy, all of this." He spread his arms as if to encompass the full aura of Rome. "It can sure play on your senses."

"I know what you mean, but those thoughts actually began on the plane coming over."

"How's that?"

"You remember that first day we met. I mentioned a boy who loved poetry."

"I do. I think I suggested a long forgotten love."

"Yes, you did. Well, he was hardly forgotten. I thought about him during much of the flight. That too, goes back to the conversation at the airport. When I talked with my friend, I told her about an unforgettable moment I'd shared with him during high school." She sighed. "I described it as the most romantic moment in my life."

"That long ago… and you never forgot it?"

"No, I couldn't." Jenny shook her head. "Isn't that something."

"Not really," John said as he looked into her eyes. "Matters of the heart are not governed by time."

"You are so right," Jenny replied. "Looking back, he was probably the love of my life."

"Did he know it?"

Jenny shook her head. "He was the boy I told you about last night…the one I wanted to marry." Jenny shrugged her shoulders. "I wanted to tell him…I came so close…."

John remained silent.

When Jenny spoke again there was a hint of cheerfulness in her voice. "My friend suggested I still might meet someone. At the time I dismissed it, but when I stepped off the plane, the Italian air must have hit me. I felt like it could still happen."

She lowered her eyes as she posed the thought, fully cognizant she was not speaking the words randomly into the air but directing them at the person sitting across from her. Then raising her eyes to his level, she spoke, hopeful her words would convey the message of her heart. "I might still meet someone like that boy."

For many seconds, they were silent, eyes searching one another. Finally, John looked away. He was not ready for this, the return of those feelings—the ones he had after her kiss on New Year's Eve and then again last night, their final evening in Venice.

His mind raced back to the resolution he had reached...

After he had left Elaine at her hotel room door, his euphoric state extended into the wee hours of the night but had ended in regret. He'd awakened to a barrage of painful questions. *Why dancing 'till midnight? Why romantic talk at Elaine's door? Why nurture my feelings about her, deep into the night?* Guilt clenched his heart at his unfaithfulness to Claire's memory, and he reminded himself again, *Romantics are forever people*. The words made him feel better, cementing his resolve. *Elaine can never be more than a friend. I must keep her at a distance.* He shook his head. *I can't deal with these feelings.*

While he dressed before breakfast, he felt better as a solution came. *All I have to be concerned about is the trip back to Rome. Of course I'll need to sit by her. I don't want to hurt her feelings, since we've been sitting together every day. But then I'll spend the afternoon by myself at the Catacombs, find a place to eat and return to the hotel. The next day I'll board the plane for home—and safety.* He breathed a sigh, the guilt was gone.

Their bus trip back had been the usual blast—laughing, joking, swapping stories. All interspersed with anecdotes of places they had visited in Verona and Venice. Unable to trust his emotions, John had looked at Bud or Kay most of the time, hoping Elaine didn't notice. Finally, on the way to San Calisto he was able to relax in the cab, feeling his plan successfully accomplished.

Then at the Catacombs, waiting for the tour to begin, everything changed when he looked up to see Elaine's face. His surprise quickly turned to exhilaration. He was thrilled she was there. Soon they were holding hands, walking down the Appian Way, seeing the fountains of Rome together...

And now—at the end of the day—she looked at him through flickering candlelight.

Oh, those eyes!

To break the spell, he propped his elbows on the table and rested his chin on his hands, (something his mother had taught him never to do). He looked down, closed his eyes and pleaded for some diversionary thought to shatter the uncomfortable silence.

Jenny, he thought to himself, *I'll talk about Jenny*. It had worked before in the aftermath of the millennium kiss, when he had used remembrances of his first love to drive out the strong feelings he was having for this woman who now sat across the table. *Maybe it will work again.*

John lifted his head and leaned back in his chair, determined to maximize the distance between them. Revealing his long kept secret, hidden from others since the day he recited the poem to Jenny in the ninth grade, filled him with excitement.

"Elaine, you want to hear a coincidence?"

JENNY KISSED ME!

"Sure."

"Guess how I spent most of my flight."

Jenny's eyes sparkled, as she guessed his thoughts. "Not you too. Tell me about it," she urged, reading the confirmation on his face.

"Yes, there was a girl in high school—" He stopped abruptly, suddenly afraid of the emotions buried with the secret.

Jenny, as if sensing his struggle, placed her hand on his. "I can tell you loved her."

Encouraged by her touch, he said wistfully, "I guess she was always there…even when I thought there was only Claire."

He looked up, as if beckoning a scene from heaven. "It happened the first time I saw her." When his eyes returned, his face glowed with a radiance which covered his whole countenance.

A few seconds later, John was laughing. "Craziness! Acting like a moonstruck teenager."

"You're just a romantic," Jenny said. "And you haven't forgotten."

"Do you want to know why?"

"Please."

"It was like Dante seeing Beatrice. You remember he was only nine when he saw her, and the effect of it remained with him the rest of his life. Well… I was fourteen."

"Tell me about it?"

"OK, first let me share what that experience came to mean to me. When I was a junior in college, I read Dante's Divine Comedy. It opened a concept of romantic love that's fascinated me ever since. You want to hear about it?"

"As long as you get back to the girl."

"I intend to. Beatrice, Dante, and the girl all connect. She was my first experience with Eros."

"Eros? I don't know if I want to hear about this."

"I know where you're coming from. You're thinking like Max."

"Max?"

"He was a guy I sat next to on the plane. He's the one who starting me thinking about this girl during the flight. We were discussing C. S. Lewis' *The Four Loves*, and we got bogged down on Eros. Ever read Lewis' book?"

"No." Jenny shook her head. "Apparently Max hadn't either."

"Do you want to hear this or not?"

"May I be excused to go to the ladies room?"

"No, you've got to learn to hold it." John touched Jenny's, hand and smiled. "Relax, this is G-rated stuff. Well, at least it's not R-rated."

"Are you sure?"

"Trust me. Eros is not sexual in nature. At least it wasn't originally. As soon as Max found that out he went to sleep." John winked. "Eros is about *being* in love. Have you heard of Charles Williams?"

Jenny shook her head.

"He connects big-time with this concept of romantic love. He was a member of the Inklings, a literary circle that included Lewis, along with others like Tolkien. You know about him, I'm sure."

"*The Hobbit, Lord of the Rings*...I've read them all."

"Well, Williams influenced both men. Anyway in the 1940s, he penned a small book entitled *The Theology of Romantic Love*. It featured Dante and Beatrice. I read it the semester I studied Dante. Here's the thesis: We can experience God in romantic love."

Jenny feigned a skeptical look. "I can understand why Max had a problem with this."

"I never got around to this part. Max was already asleep, remember?"

"Sorry, I forgot."

"Here's the idea, Elaine. We can discover something of the nature of God in the falling-in-love experience. When Dante met Beatrice he encountered perfection. She was the image of love, beauty, and goodness. When she smiled, the effect on him was profound. In Beatrice's presence, he knew only absolute good will toward all. Williams refers to it as *Charitas*."

"And the girl affected you that way?"

"Yes." John paused, his face lighting up from the thought. "When I first saw her it had the same effect. I was at an all-time low in my life. The world had fallen in on me. I had lost my dad and was among strangers in a new town. I didn't want to be around anyone. Suddenly—there she was—and my feelings completely changed. It was blissful."

Jenny lit up. "I get it. As I once heard a professor say on Ponte Vecchio, 'experiencing human love could guide one ultimately to God.'"

John looked amazed. "Almost perfect recall. I wish I had more students like you."

Elaine faked a smile, impishly fluttered her eyes, and said, "I wish I'd had more professors like you."

He grinned. "Now, you didn't need to find refuge in the ladies room after all, did you?"

Jenny ignored his question and pleaded, "Now, back to the girl. Did she ever know how you felt about her?"

"I tried to tell her a few weeks after I saw her that first time." He shook his head. "I think the feelings were all one-sided." John sipped his coffee. Ice cold. It didn't matter, he was lost in thought. He relished the moment, telling someone about Jenny after all the years of silence.

Jenny interrupted the lull. "Whatcha thinking about?"

"Oh, sorry," John said, jolted back to their conversation. "I was thinking about her…and Philia. It's also one of the four loves. We did experience that. It was our senior year."

Jenny's eyebrows raised. "Philia?"

"Friendship." John explained. "It's that special bond two people can share."

"Like Frank Sinatra and Dean Martin?" Jenny grinned.

John chuckled. "I was really looking for an illustration with a little more vintage than the Rat Pack."

"Oh, I know. I can't believe I didn't think of this—*the statue*."

"The statue…what do you mean?"

JENNY KISSED ME!

"In Florence…David and Jonathan."

"Oh yes, that's a great example. It's one of the most famous friendships in history."

"I love that name."

"David?"

"No…Jonathan."

"Really, I went by that name during my school years."

"I'm not surprised, you seem like a Jonathan." Jenny's eyes sparkled. "May I call you that?"

His look expressed approval. "Claire always did. She—"

His words were drowned out by the familiar strains of a popular Italian song, "Arrivederci Roma," sung by the restaurant serenader. It filled the air, as many of the customers joined in singing. John and Jenny did not. Neither of their hearts welcomed the lyrics, which spoke of saying goodbye and parting.

As they glanced from the serenader to one another, there was sadness brought on by a shared memory of long ago. Had either been able to picture the scene in the others' mind, it would have taken them to the same time and place—graduation day when only their eyes had said goodbye.

Grateful when the song ended, John welcomed a cue from several customers nearby who got up from their table. "I guess it's that time. By tomorrow—" John looked at his watch and caught himself, "I mean today—"

Jenny broke in. "What a lovely evening." Then sensing the inadequacy of her words, she added, "A perfect evening, Jonathan."

Her thoughts turned inward as she got up. Jenny didn't look at John while they returned to their cab. She wanted to be alone to reflect on a word she had spoken—*Jonathan.* The name had come out so naturally. A thought overwhelmed her. *Jonathan is out there somewhere...surely thousands of miles away. Wherever he is...he's just like this man I've come to love. It's been like going home.*

EIGHTEEN

Going Home

The twosome engaged in small talk until John walked Jenny to her room. Stopping at her door, he gently clasped her shoulders.

"Elaine, this has been wonderful here in Italy…and today has been the best… a real memory day." He looked deeply into her eyes. "You made it so." Leaning forward, he kissed her on the forehead, embraced her tightly and bid her goodnight. He started to walk away but turned abruptly. "I wish it wasn't going to end tomorrow." Then he headed to his room.

Dismayed by his quick departure, Jenny's eyes followed him down the hallway, as she said softly, "Goodnight, Jonathan." She doubted he heard her.

When his door closed, she turned and walked down the hall.

An hour later, she returned to her room and headed for the nearest chair. It was late, almost two, and she was faced with a decision. First, she poured over the highlights of the day—the best since she landed in Italy, just her and Jonathan. It was idyllic.

Jenny revisited their surprise meeting at the catacombs, their walk hand in hand down the Appian Way, viewing the fountains, and sharing memories of their first loves during the candlelight dinner. Throughout the day, they had been absorbed in each other—eyes, thoughts, being. She replayed the final scene, first his words—"a memory day…you made it so", then his arms around her and his kiss. She had so longed for his touch, and it brought a perfect ending to the day.

In retrospect, from their first meeting at the Spanish Steps, Jenny had felt an inexplicable bond—never more apparent than today. But the ecstasy was interrupted with the reality of his words, "I wish it wasn't going to end tomorrow."

In a few hours, the sun would rise on their last day in Italy. She would fly back to Texas. Jonathan would leave for Arizona. The final hours had arrived so suddenly. Their time together had been like a dream. But the dream was ending, and once again, words were left unspoken.

It was like 1960, all over again—the senior prom, graduation day, but another Jonathan. Her emotions and failure to express them were eerily the same.

This time she would break the silence and speak her feelings. She looked at her watch. There was still an opportunity. Their group always met for breakfast. It was only five hours away.

She hastily settled on a plan. It was simple. It was direct. It was honest. This time, she would be true to herself. She thought of how Kay had revealed her heart to Bud, and that gave her courage. After breakfast, she would ask Jonathan to walk her back to her room, and then invite him inside. Once they entered, she would tell him what had been in her heart since they stood side by side on the Ponte Vecchio, look into his eyes, and say, "Jonathan…I love you."

His response could mean a new life—a life she once let slip away—a second chance.

For a moment, she considered the unthinkable. *What if Jonathan says nothing? What if he does nothing?* She didn't dwell on it long. The thought was unbearable. Jenny knew he cared for her. Even more, she believed he loved her. But she couldn't dismiss the uneasiness that, for him, there was still Claire.

As she dressed for bed, she glanced at her watch again. Then kneeling, she said a short prayer. "Please Lord, I can't bear to lose him."

ಅಅಅ

A few minutes after seven, Jenny walked briskly to the hotel restaurant. Even with less than three hours sleep, she had awakened expectantly, assuming her brief petition was the reason for her optimism. In her estimation, everything seemed to point to a plea God would honor.

Jenny looked about as she entered the dining area. None of the foursome was there yet. The oddity struck her. Seven was their customary gathering time, and she was always the last to arrive. *They must have decided to pack before breakfast.*

She selected a table and waited a few minutes before serving herself at the buffet. The minutes crept by. Her untouched food was cold now. She watched the entrance as her optimism turned to anxiety. She checked her watch, continuing to look toward the door. It was now eight. Her anxiety turned to despair. She knew Jonathan wasn't coming. Even though Bud and Kay were not there either, his absence was what mattered to her. Her mind raced, *He knows this will be our last time together.* And then she thought again, *What if he can't let Claire go?*

An empty chair next to her delivered the painful answer.

Jenny's emotions plunged as she accepted the inconceivable. Feeling weak, she placed both hands on the table as she rose, and then she walked in a daze toward the lobby. Determined to avoid other tour members before the tears flowed, she summoned the energy to make a dash for the elevator and then walk back to her room.

ৡৡৡ

It was also a near sleepless night for John. At 6 a.m., he dressed and walked down the hall to see Bud. John normally didn't knock on hotel doors at that hour, but Bud had mentioned he was an early riser, and John needed to talk. He too, was faced with a decision, and based on a past experience, he knew it could have a momentous consequence.

One question occupied his mind. *What will I say to Elaine—it's our final day together?* Those initial stirrings of love he felt that last evening in Venice, fueled by the beautiful day they spent together in Rome consumed him. There was no denying the reality—he loved Elaine.

Before he reached Bud's room, John stopped in his tracks and envisioned a scene from forty years ago—a girl in her cap and gown looking up at him. He imagined Jenny as clearly as if it were yesterday, when he longed to say he loved her. But instead he had walked away, never speaking to her again. Now he wanted to tell Elaine the same thing, but a haunting thought which had kept him awake much of the night was still there. *How can I let Claire go?*

He knocked on Bud's door and was greeted by a seemingly perturbed figure. "You selling pizza, Professor? I don't eat it this early in the morning."

"Bud, are you game for a cup of coffee?"

"You're on. Wait a minute, Kay is still in bed. Let me give her a quick kiss and tell her where I'm headed." Two minutes later Bud returned with some good news. "I just noticed it's after six. We won't have to go out. We can catch the buffet downstairs. You can buy me coffee some other time…in Indiana."

They walked down the stairway leading to the breakfast dining room. Soon the two friends filled their plates, poured their coffee, and sat down. They were all alone in the room.

Noticing the emptiness, Bud said, "Most tourists have sense enough to sleep late on their vacations, especially when they're up late into the night…right?"

"How'd you guess?"

"Not a toughie. You look like you've been up all night, my friend. Although that's not the only reason I guessed it. I know you have something heavy weighing on your mind. That tends to cut into sleep time."

"If you're such a mind reader, tell me what it is?"

"Elaine."

"Does it show?"

"We're in Rome…is the Pope Catholic?"

"Did you know we spent yesterday afternoon and evening together?"

"Uh-huh. Kay and I figured it out when we couldn't find either of you around the hotel. Then Elaine showed up at our door after you left her last night and confirmed our suspicion."

Bud's look prompted John to ask, "Is there something I should know about why she was there?"

"I think you could say that. She woke us up to talk about the same thing you're here to talk to me about." Bud sipped his coffee. "You know the topic, right?"

John looked down at his plate and mumbled, "Us…I suppose."

Bud's demeanor changed. "You *suppose*? John, I've been calling you Professor since shortly after we met, but I equate your profession with being smart, and you aren't being nearly as swift between the ears as I think you ought to be. You seem to be missing what's going on here."

"Go on...I've never seen you this serious. I'm intrigued."

Bud leaned forward. "Elaine's in love with you, and you're in love with her. *She* knows it.... *You* know it.... And *Kay* knows it. Now I could attribute that to the fact you three are a bunch of romantics, and you're letting Italy get to you. But there is nothing maudlin about me. I'm a practical, unsentimental, building contractor, whose heart is still in Hoosier land. And even I know you two are in love."

John rubbed his hand across his forehead as he listened, then glanced away from Bud's penetrating eyes.

"Bud there's more to it."

"You mean Claire."

John's eyes quickly darted back to Bud.

"So," Bud continued, "that's it. Has to be. There's no other possibility."

John sighed. "Bud, when Claire died, I knew I could never marry again. It wasn't even a consideration, not for a single moment. Then I come over here for eight days—eight days—and I decide to forget that?" He hesitated, shook his head, and then said, "I have my teaching, Bud. I love it. That should be enough."

Bud countered, "A perceptive fellow can learn a lot in eight days. During that period, you've learned that what you thought was enough is not enough. You need Elaine, and she needs you. My idea of an educated person is someone who is open to new possibilities and new ways of looking at things. You need to wise up, associate professor."

John managed a chuckle. "You demoted me."

"Yes, and I'm afraid you could end up in grade school before this conversation is over. John, here's something you need to think about. You've told me enough about Claire that I feel like I know her. So ask yourself. What would Claire want you to do? Would she want you to spend your life grieving over her, or would she want you to have the happiness you can have with someone as wonderful as Elaine? I think I know the answer, but the ball's in your court."

John stared at his coffee cup. Then he gripped it tight, stood up, and walked over to the buffet for a refill. Returning, he put the cup back down and started to speak, but the words clogged in his throat. Taking a deep breath, he made a second attempt. "It's so hard to let Claire go. *Romantics are forever people.*"

Bud took a deep breath and exhaled. "I know...I know. I'm married to one."

Bud produced a pen and a small notepad from his shirt pocket. He wrote something down and turned to John. "Would you do this for me?" he pleaded. "I want you to take a long walk...very long. You've got some thinking to do about your life together with Claire, and the question I asked about what she would want you to do. Then here's my next favor. I want you to think about this lovely woman God brought into your life." Bud cleared his throat and continued in his serious tone. "John, you believe in Providence, don't you?"

John nodded.

"Perhaps it's time for you to make new memories." Bud paused. "Elaine would be someone to make them with."

JENNY KISSED ME!

Tearing the page out of the notepad, Bud folded it and handed it to John. "End your walk here. You'll know the answer."

John stood up to leave, pausing to peek at the scrawled words on the paper. Then he spun around. "You big fake, get up."

"Are you going to hit me?"

"You're too big to hit. You're not too big to hug…you unsentimental building contractor."

୨୧୨୧୨୧

Jenny rubbed her eyes, aware of the clock sitting on the dresser. Twelve noon. She had cried herself back to sleep. She thought momentarily about walking to Bud and Kay's room but nixed the idea, realizing their presence would only revive the tears it had taken so long to extinguish. In fact, Jenny didn't want to see anyone. She wanted to be on a plane headed to New Jersey and leave Italy far behind.

Turning her thoughts to the flight home, for the first time, she remembered Sandra and exclaimed, "Oh, my, I totally forgot. I promised I'd call her from Italy!"

She glanced at the clock again, and made a quick calculation. *It's 5 a.m. in Newark. Sandra will probably still be asleep, so I'll keep it brief. At least, it will please her that I remembered.*

She bolstered her spirits for the impending conversation. *Sandra can't know that I've failed again.* She dialed the phone and waited.

A sleepy sounding Sandra picked up the receiver. "Hello."

"*Buongiorno* from Rome. Guess who?" Jenny responded with feigned cheerfulness.

"Umm…it's about time. Three days ago I gave up on you keeping your promise. Hope it was because you were having fun."

"Sandra, I'm sorry about not calling until now. This final day in Rome is really the only free time I've had."

"Well? Did you have a good time?"

"Yes, it's been a neat trip. I can't wait to tell you all about it. My plane gets in about eight this evening. You have the flight number. I'm really looking forward to spending time with you."

"Me too, I've got the guest room ready."

"Sandra, since we're going to be up late talking this evening, I'll let you get back to sleep now."

"Jenny before you go let me tell you something. If I don't do it now, I'll probably forget."

"What is it?"

"Yesterday I was thinking about you and remembered our talk at the airport."

"Un-huh?

"I located our high school annual, and looked up that boy."

"You looked up what boy?"

"What boy? The one you told me about at the airport. I couldn't forget about him and the poem. Remember, you had forgotten his last name. Do you still want to know it?"

"Oh, I guess. What was it?"

"It was Kaelin…Jonathan Kaelin."

"*Kaelin? Kaelin?*"

JENNY KISSED ME!

"Yes, Jonathan Kaelin."

"Jenny, can you hear me? Are you still on the line?"

"Are you sure it was *Jonathan Kaelin*?" Jenny replied in a shaky voice.

"Yes, I'm sure...Jenny what's wrong...! Jenny...! Jenny...!"

The last words Jenny heard before she dropped the phone were "I'm sure." She burst out of her room, raced to John's door and began knocking, each knock louder than before. No response, so she headed for Kay and Bud's room, whispering, "Please be there, somebody please be there."

Her plea was answered when Bud opened the door.

"Come in, we were just on our way to see you. You saved us a trip."

Then perceiving Jenny was about to explode, Bud asked, "What's happened?"

"Do you know where John is from?"

"What! You've got to be kidding. In the midst of all that poetry nonsense, you never got around to asking? He's from Arizona."

"Arizona, I know about Arizona. He has taught there for thirty years. But do you know where he *grew up*?"

"Wait," she raised her hand. "If you know, and it wasn't Arizona...just nod your head, but please...don't tell me...not yet."

Puzzled, Bud slowly nodded.

Jenny closed her eyes and took a deep breath. Then she blurted out, "Alright, I'm ready. You can tell me."

"He's from Texas, same as you."

253

Jenny's heart beat faster as the pieces started to fit. Even so, it was too much to believe. Surely, it couldn't be true. She tried to remain calm, afraid to build her hopes.

"Elaine, you didn't know that? All this Texas braggadocio we hear about, and he never mentioned it? And neither did you?"

"I never asked him," Jenny replied impatiently. "I assumed he had always lived in Arizona. He knew I taught school in Dallas, but I never said anything about where I grew up. Texas is a big state, you know."

"Yes, I do. You people have a way of reminding us of that."

"You wouldn't possibly know his hometown, would you?"

"You know," Bud mused, "that first evening we had dinner with him, he told us. We talked about our vacations, including several trips to Texas. It so happened we spent a couple of days in his hometown. It's a tourist resort."

"*A tourist resort*?" Her eyes filled with tears, her voice trembled. "Can you tell me the name?"

"No, but Kay can. She never forgets that stuff."

"Where is she?"

"She's in the bathroom. You want me to beat on the door?"

Just then, Kay emerged.

"Dearie, do you remember the name of that tourist town in Texas where John grew up?"

"Yes, it was San Marcos."

Jenny's knees weakened. She staggered backward and collapsed into a nearby chair, covering her face,

JENNY KISSED ME!

sobbing and shaking uncontrollably. Kay and Bud stared, speechless.

Several minutes passed before Kay spoke. "Elaine, what's happened?"

Jenny looked up, cheeks drenched in tears. But when Kay saw the broad smile and twinkling eyes, she knew whatever had happened was wonderful.

Finally, her voice quivering, Jenny replied, "Kay, I'm sorry... I'll have to tell you later." She caught her breath. Her voice took on a sense of urgency as she spoke. "All I want now is to find Jonathan...I mean John. Do you know where he is? He's not in his room."

"He and Bud had breakfast together early this morning. Do you know, honey?"

"John left for a walk after we finished eating," Bud said, checking his watch. "If I were you, I think I'd try Trevi Fountain." Gently placing his hand on her shoulder, he added reassuringly, "Elaine, I believe he's waiting for you."

"Do you want me to call a cab?" Kay asked.

"Please."

Jenny gave Bud a quick kiss. Then turning to Kay, she hugged her friend and whispered in her ear, "Thanks...for remembering the town."

Bud opened the door and said, "Elaine, don't let him get away."

Jenny stopped abruptly when she entered the hall then turned and stepped back into their room. She reached out and took hold of both of their hands. "John is someone I loved in high school, but I let him get away. It won't happen this time."

As she walked away, she turned and smiled at her bewildered friends. "I'll fill in the details later."

ം‑ം‑ം

After wandering the streets of Rome for hours, thinking first of Claire and then Elaine, John arrived at the place he knew his struggle must be resolved. Of all the locations in Rome, Claire's memory was strongest at Trevi Fountain. Bud had not known that, but his romantic instincts had directed John to the perfect spot.

A mist began falling as John approached. He was pleased. The weather would keep the crowd down. Following his friend's request, John had saved the question for now. To answer it meant he had to return to a painful time—one he had driven from his mind moments after it took place…

It was three weeks prior to Claire's death, shortly after the return home from her final stay in the hospital. John was sitting by her on the bed during lunch. He started to return the tray of scarcely touched food, when Claire placed her hand on his. "Jonathan I want to talk about something that's difficult for me, but we've never hidden our thoughts from one another." She paused. "When we first heard my diagnosis, we turned it over to God." Gripping his hand a little tighter she added, "We both know I'm going to die. I don't want to leave you and the children yet—" her eyes begin to tear up— "or the grandchildren. But you understand…I am at peace, and I look forward to seeing the Lord."

Her voice grew weaker. "There'll be no passage of time where I'm going…but Jonathan, there will be for you." Then sitting up in bed, she leaned over, held John's face between her hands and said, "I want you to do something for me. It's on my last honey-do list." She smiled. "Jonathan, I hope you can marry again." She placed her hand on his mouth. "No, don't say anything now. Someday in the months ahead, after I'm gone, I want you to remember this moment, and what I asked of you. You are too wonderful a man to spend the rest of your years alone. If God brings someone into your life, to share what I've known for these thirty-three years…remember my wish." Then removing her hand from his lips, she replaced it with a kiss…

John stood at the rail for some time, remembering her wish and looking at the fountain through tears, until finally his sorrow was gone, and a wave of peace covered him.

"Goodbye, Claire…. I love you." He wiped away the tears and smiled.

ৡৡৡ

The mist turned into a light rain, and the few people who had been at Trevi were gone. John was indifferent to the weather. His heart had been unleashed by the memory of Claire's wish. But before he was completely free, there was a final matter—his wedding ring. He looked down at his finger where Claire had placed the ring so many years ago. It had not been off his finger in over thirty years, not since he heard those words accompanying the ring ceremony. "*This ring I give to you in token and pledge of our abiding love.*" Touching the ring lightly with his fingers, he slowly removed it and held it briefly. Then John slipped it into his trouser pocket. Now he was ready. His attention turned toward finding Elaine.

As he turned to take his first step, he noticed movement in the distance. John rubbed his eyes once again. It was not wishful thinking; it was Elaine coming slowly toward him.

John began walking to meet her, when Elaine suddenly thrust her palms forward in a halting manner. He had already slowed his steps to a near stop, captivated by her appearance.

Elaine's face was radiant.

"Jonathan, before you come any closer, I have something to say to you. I've been waiting over *forty* years to say it."

John stopped instantly—mystified.

"I have a question about poetry. Tell me who wrote these words:

> Believe me if all those endearing young charms,
> Which I gaze on so fondly to-day,
> Were to change by to-morrow, and fleet in my arms,
> Like fairy-gifts fading away,
> Thou wouldst still be adored, as this moment thou art,
> Let thy loveliness fade as it will…"

Growing more perplexed by the second, John managed a halting answer. "Thomas Moore…it's a favorite of mine, but I don't understand—"

JENNY KISSED ME!

Jenny interrupted, smiling. "Don't you *know*, Jonathan? Don't you *remember*?"

"Remember?"

"Let me tell you a story about that poem. A long time ago, in a town called San Marcos, in the Texas hill country, *a fourteen year old boy named Jonathan Kaelin wrote it for* a fourteen year old girl named Jennifer Elaine Nichols."

John stared at her, spellbound.

Jenny stepped nearer. "You see, you were wrong about that girl you spoke of last night. She did love you." Tears trickled down her cheeks, but her eyes sparkled. "When Jonathan spoke those words to her in English class, he won her heart. She kept it secret all those years in school."

He started to speak, but the words stuck in his throat. Finally, he managed a barely audible, "I never knew." He repeated the words only this time his voice trembled as he spoke her name. "Jenny, Oh Jenny…I never knew."

"I know…I couldn't tell you, Jonathan…Now I can."

Clasping both hands over her heart, she looked at him adoringly and whispered, "You were always here."

The sight was too much for John to restrain the tears. As they had earlier flowed with memories of Claire, they flowed again. Only this time they were tears of joy—unbelievable, impossible joy.

"Jonathan, remember the promise in the poem:

It is not while beauty and youth are thine own,
And thy cheeks unprofaned by a tear,

That the fervor and faith of a soul may be known,
To which time will but make thee more dear!"

Jenny's eyes searched. "Do you still mean it? I'm not a girl anymore, Jonathan.... I'm not as pretty as I used to be...and the tears—" Jenny touched her cheeks as tears merged indiscernibly with the falling raindrops.

John gazed in wonder, imploring the rain not to wash this moment away as if it were a fleeting dream. He managed to nod several times. "I do."

"Jonathan, that day in the library...that one moment she revealed her heart. You remember what she did?"

It was as if her words had magically transferred the scene to Jonathan. His eyes took on a faraway look.

She continued speaking softly, "What if the girl who kissed that boy in the library had not walked away? What would he have done?"

Jonathan closed the narrow space separating them, reached out his hand, and gently touched Jenny's shoulder. She was no dream, she was real. This was his moment. He could finally speak the words so long concealed in his heart. Looking into her eyes, he drew her to him and finally shared his secret. "I love you Jenny, I've always loved you." He smiled. "Elaine."

They held each other tight, as if both had found a long lost treasure. Closing his eyes, Jonathan turned his face up into the rain. His dream was about to come true, and he had to visit the scene one final time—the place where it had been planted so many years ago. There she was in the cafeteria. She was fourteen again with long black hair…falling against her red sweater…and she was smiling. Recapturing the feeling of that moment, he cupped Jenny's rain soaked hair in his hands and began kissing each tear…or was it the raindrops. It didn't matter. They rested on the most beautiful face he had ever seen.

"My Jenny. Your loveliness has not faded." Then he tenderly kissed her lips, once, twice.

Drawing his head back, Jonathan looked at her once more, and saw the smile. It really was her. Their lips met again, but this time, many raindrops fell before they parted. Jonathan had dreamed of this moment a thousand times back in high school. His dreams were sweet; the reality sweeter still.

At last, Jenny was his.

಄಄಄

Though the hotel was almost a mile away, there was no desire for a cab. Ignoring the rain, they walked, silently, hand in hand. Ever so often, they would glance at one another, knowing instinctively what the other was thinking. Finally, Jonathan voiced their thoughts, "Is this really happening?"

She leaned up to the very spot on his cheek that her lips had touched over forty years ago. The answer was in Jenny's kiss.

Acknowledgment

A serendipity which came about as a result of writing this novel was that it brought me into contact with one of the most remarkable people I have ever met.

Mike LeFan of Temple, TX contracted polio in the early 1950s at the age of eight. From that time on, he spent nights in an iron lung. When the sun rose to beckon a new day, Mike greeted it with a portable respirator. The disease left him almost completely paralyzed. All he could move were the toes on his left foot, but he took the lemon life had given him and made lemonade. Mike could draw, paint, and type 40 words a minute on his computer. After getting a college degree, he started his own business as a freelance writer and editor. It was in the latter capacity that I came to know him. Mike's contribution to Jenny Kissed Me! was inestimable through the first twelve chapters. He did not finish chapter thirteen. In March of 2013, at the age of 67, he left his iron lung for the environs of heaven. I miss him.

Made in the USA
Charleston, SC
11 September 2014